THE OLD FIRE

ELISA SHUA DUSAPIN

TRANSLATED BY ANEESA ABBAS HIGGINS

This edition first published in the United Kingdom in 2026 by
Daunt Books Originals
83 Marylebone High Street
London W1U 4QW
publishing@dauntbooks.co.uk

1

Copyright © 2023, Éditions Zoé
Published by arrangement with Agence littéraire Astier-Pécher

English translation copyright © 2026, Aneesa Abbas Higgins
With the support of the Swiss Arts Council Pro Helvetia

First published in French as *Le Vieil Incendie* by Éditions Zoé, 2023

The right of Elisa Shua Dusapin to be identified as the author
of this work has been asserted by her in accordance with the
Copyright, Designs and Patents Act 1988

The right of Aneesa Abbas Higgins to be identified as the
translator of this work has been asserted by her in accordance
with the Copyright, Designs and Patents Act 1988

All rights reserved. No part of this publication may be reproduced,
stored in a retrieval system, copied or transmitted, in any form
or by any means without the prior written permission of
Daunt Books, nor be otherwise circulated in any form of binding
or cover other than that in which it is published and without a
similar condition being imposed on the subsequent purchaser.

A CIP catalogue record for this title
is available from the British Library.

ISBN 978-1-917092-33-3

Typeset by Marsha Swan
Printed and bound in Great Britain by Clays Ltd, Elcograf S.p.A.

www.dauntbookspublishing.co.uk

For my sisters

THE
OLD FIRE

6 NOVEMBER

The rain was coming down so hard I missed the sign for the village. It had smudged the tyre tracks, flattened out the ruts. In the end I couldn't see where I was going and had to pull over to the side of the road. All that water hammering down on the bonnet. It started raining yesterday and hasn't stopped. I haven't seen a soul since I left the autoroute. There were warnings on the radio not to drive but I didn't have any choice. It's evening now, seven o'clock, the sky almost black. I haven't worked out how to adjust the angle of the seat, so I'm sitting upright, waiting, stunned by the noise of the rain.

At least the rental van I'm driving seems solid. It looks a bit like a road-sweeper van, orange-coloured. I told the hire company I wanted something practical.

An hour goes by. At last the downpour begins to ease. I turn the key in the ignition. The satnav leads me deeper into the forest. Before long, the canopy is so dense that neither rain nor light can penetrate. I switch the headlights to full beam. It's hard to steer. I drive slowly for several kilometres, guessing at the position of the track beneath the undergrowth. Eventually I emerge at the foot of a steep slope. Above me the familiar sight of the gates at the top of the slope comes into view. I put the van into first gear and gun the engine, just as my father used to do. I've never done this before. The tyres skid over the rocky terrain but the van holds the road. The gates are open and I pull in and stop in front of the house. I turn off the ignition. The security lighting comes on. A rabbit scampers into the undergrowth.

The building looks tired, the ivy-covered roof sagging above the brickwork, like a weary giant gasping for breath. There's a car parked under the hazelnut tree. Bracken forces its way between the cracks in the front steps. Through the window, I can see a light inside. I press one eye to the spy hole in the front door and immediately pull away. I wasn't expecting to see my sister's face, fish-eyed, her forehead enlarged, eyebrows spread, her features magnified by the lens. My father installed it the wrong way round, deliberately, he claimed. We had nothing to hide, he said, no reason to be afraid. We had inner riches and the whole world should know that this was the home of the most beautiful people.

'Hi!' I say as Véra opens the door. I sound like I'm shouting. Véra grins in response, her smile too wide for her mouth. She takes my suitcase from my hand, puts it down by the stairs in the kitchen. It's all so familiar, the stone floor, the wooden furniture, the bathroom door almost hidden by the fireplace. The chimney is stopped up, the fireplace filled with books. That's new. A birdcage hangs above the table, where the light fixture used to be, slabs of cheese visible through the bars.

Véra points at the stairs, then indicates that she's working at the kitchen counter, I should get settled in while she puts the final touches to the meal. She seems very organised, she used to be so chaotic. I say something complimentary. She types on her phone, shows me the screen:

To make you feel welcome.

I reply curtly that we're sisters, it's my home too, we don't need to stand on ceremony. She lights the gas hurriedly.

'Especially since we're not keeping any of this stuff,' I say, unable to stop myself.

My socks make a swishing sound on the stairs. I tread carefully, not wanting to slip. The door to our parents' bedroom is open. I stand on the threshold, feeling the draught from the poorly sealed French doors. Dark wood flooring. The double bed in the centre of the room, the mattress bare, stripped of sheets and blankets. I still don't understand how my parents managed to sleep without a wall behind their heads. I close the door, feeling vaguely relieved. I'm not sure what had been worrying me the most, the thought of sleeping in their bed or the prospect of sharing our old room with my sister. We're not children anymore.

Her sickly-sweet perfume irritates my throat. She's kept our bunk beds. The sight of them makes me feel sad. The metal frame seems too fragile to support two fully grown women. The bureau and chest of drawers haven't moved, still salmon pink, their rounded shapes the same as ever.

I check my internet connection. I'm going to be here for nine days, I need to be able to communicate with my colleagues. My phone shows only one bar, sometimes none at all.

Leaning out of the window I can see the van. The orange colour makes me laugh, it looks like a giant bumble-bee. How absurd. The whole situation is absurd, my sister and I together again like this for the first time since my father died five years ago.

Downstairs, Véra has poured two glasses of wine. She's used the crystal glasses. I'm so put off by all this formality that I tell her I don't drink. She raises an eyebrow, pours the wine back into the bottle, spilling some of it onto the table. I wipe it away with my sleeve. All of a sudden I feel hot and decide to take off my jumper. Bamboo dishes. I haven't seen those before. Véra shows me the packaging for the cheese, decorated with chestnuts, then points proudly to the fireplace. Smoked cheese. I try not to think about it being made with raw milk. She's made an endive salad with figs and walnuts. I ask her if she's given any thought to how we're going to approach the task of emptying the house over the next few days. I haven't had a moment to plan, I've been so busy. She types out:

`Well done for your prize.`

I mumble that it's kind of her to remember.

I'm curious as to how she knows about the prize. I write film scripts for a living. The latest won a prize recently at a festival in Italy. I didn't go to the festival and I certainly wouldn't have said anything to Véra about it.

'Have you heard anything from Octave?' I ask her in what I hope is a neutral voice.

She nods, yes, of course – the figs, the walnuts, they're from him. I don't wait for her to finish. As far as I'm concerned, I say, there's nothing I want to keep from the house. She can sort out the things she wants for herself and we'll take the rest to the tip. Her fingers tighten around her phone. She tilts her chin in the direction of the armoire, the kitchen, the bathroom. I look up. We're not going to sort through all that, are we? The phone's screen throws light on her face.

`Up to you.`

I feel myself starting to relax a little. It's just that I have a lot of work right now, I tell her. I've fallen behind. I'll need some time alone to write while I'm here. She points at the screen again:

Up to you.

She makes it all seem so simple, it's disconcerting. Then she asks me what I've been up to. I say something about my latest commission, adapting Georges Perec's novel, *W or the Memory of Childhood*. Véra listens, smiling as I speak. I hint at the prestige of this production, doing my best to appear nonchalant about the famous actors lined up, the well-known screenwriters I'm working with. We have six episodes to write. Filming is due to begin in two years. Applause from Véra. It's not an easy work to adapt, I add. And I'm only involved in the dialogue. I start to say something about Perec, she nods vigorously, yes, she knows, she's read *A Void*.

'You read things like that?'

She pulls a face, of course she does.

'I don't know. My father . . .'

Silence.

'Papa, I mean. He didn't say.'

Still smiling, Véra serves me the last of the figs.

I was fifteen when I left for the US. Véra was twelve. I went there for high school and lived with a host family. Véra had stopped speaking long before I left. I knew that she managed to keep up at school most of the time but I'd assumed her reading hadn't progressed beyond a basic level. I certainly didn't think she'd be up to reading Perec.

'What about you? How are things with you?' I say, realising that I haven't asked her about herself once since I arrived. The last time we communicated was a year ago when she moved to Périgueux. She'd been living in this house, our childhood home, with my father and stayed on after he passed away. Last year she found a furnished studio flat and I'd been giving her advice at long distance. She tells me she didn't take anything from the house – she didn't want to take things without my approval. Now that the sale of the house has been finalised, she is counting on me to help her clear it out.

I'm reading over her shoulder. She gestures annoyance, tells me not to rush her. I apologise, help myself to some more salad.

Our house used to be part of the estate of neighbouring château, Le Pigeon Froid, owned by Octave's family. But the boundaries have been redrawn. The house is in need of updating. To conform to modern safety standards we'd have to redo the roof and modernise the central heating and electrical installation. We don't have the money to do any of this and we've accepted an offer from a company that wants to knock down the house and set up a campsite. Octave is hoping to salvage some of the stone from the house and use it for the restoration of the château's pigeonnier, the tower where the pigeons used to be housed.

Véra waves her phone at me. She was bored with her job working in a shop, she says. Now, she's doing a course in flower stabilisation.

'Stabilisation?'

```
I create flowers that never fade, with the
help of chemistry.
```

I give her a look that says I'm interested.

'And is it successful?'

```
It depends on the flowers.
```

'I mean commercially. Do they sell?'

She shrugs:

```
People can't be bothered anymore.
```

We clear away the dishes in silence.

'Well,' I say flatly, 'it's November. Not the best time of year for flowers.'

Véra goes straight to bed. I linger downstairs in the lounge. Darkness is encroaching, the floor lamps cast dim haloes. I feel ill at ease in their warm glow. No curtains on the windows. I see myself reflected in the glass, seated on the sofa, framed by darkness, the fridge purring in the background, the smell of cheese – Véra has put it back in its birdcage. I feel oppressed by it all, the blocked-up fireplace, the walls festooned with prints of Van Gogh's sunflowers. My father collected posters from theatre productions and art exhibitions. He had no particular interest in the artists and never went to see the plays. It was the images he loved. He chose them for their bright colours and pinned the posters up all over the house.

I feel exhausted just thinking about the task of clearing out all this mess. If we set fire to the books, there'd be nothing left. Except the stones the house is made of. They're the only things we need to preserve anyway. How much simpler that would be.

I put off sorting through my emails until tomorrow and spend the evening poring over my text messages feeling increasingly anxious as I scroll through and find none from Irvin. It's almost evening in New York, plenty of time for him to have messaged me. I'm tempted to wait until I hear from him first, then decide that would be childish.

I let him know I've arrived, say goodnight to him. I pause, hesitate for a moment, then tell him I miss him.

The bathroom is as I remember it, cavern-like with bare stone walls and floor. Véra has left a towel for me, neatly folded on the worm-eaten chest of drawers. Even though I know the wood's been treated, I've always found this chest of drawers repellent. She's left her jewellery here. Handcrafted bits and bobs, feathers, shells. I open one of the drawers. It's stuffed with amber, necklaces, brooches. Pushing the wet bathmat aside with my foot, I step into the shower and watch Véra's hair being sucked down the drain, hoping it won't cause a blockage.

I stand for a long time under the stream of scalding water. My hair is brittle, crinkled from where the elastic tie was. My hormone levels have been all over the place. I don't know when my period will start again. I turn around to face the stone wall, still instinctively looking for something to lean against and trying not to look down at my belly. Irvin claimed he didn't notice it swelling. He says it was all in my head. I know he's only trying to reassure me. I can't blame him. He didn't have to watch his insides being emptied out down his legs, turning the water red and disappearing down the pipes. He knows nothing of my body.

The harder I try not to make a sound, the more the stairs creak. The bedroom is lit by the greenish glow from our two phones charging. Véra is under the covers, only her head visible, her hands cupped on her chest. Her clothes are rolled up on the chest of drawers. The ladder to the top bunk squeaks, the sheets make a rustling sound. I fall asleep instantly, bathed in the smell of fresh laundry.

7 NOVEMBER

I'm sorting things into categories – items to be thrown out, those to be given away. I can't help smiling as I realise I'm following the advice of decluttering influencers. A cold light filters in through the window. Spiders are clustered in corners and all around the stove. They don't seem to have spun any webs. I find dead ones in pots and pans and dispose of them. I've decided to start in the kitchen, somehow it has fewer associations than other rooms. Anything that's passed its sell-by date goes straight into a bin bag. Mustard, tomato concentrate. A jar with a lump of something white – duck fat.

A whole shelf of cheeses. The fridge shudders as I launch my attack. The freezer compartment needs defrosting. The plastic has cracks in it. Since she moved out, Véra's only been back here once a month. Potatoes in the vegetable drawer have sprouted. The smell from the cheese makes me feel nauseous. I work quickly. Mouldy jam, almost empty packets of butter, bunches of wilted herbs.

Véra is busy in our bedroom. Her presence in the house unsettles me. I listen for sounds from her. She came downstairs a little while ago to make herself some coffee just as I was sniffing a jar of stewed fruit. She asked me if I wanted some. I didn't know if she meant coffee or stewed fruit and dumped the jar of fruit into the bin, like a rabbit caught in the headlights throwing itself under the car.

Véra's making progress too. I'm worried we're going to end up having too much time on our hands. What will I do with her for another six days? I make a conscious effort to work more slowly.

The kitchen is a mess. It looks more like the Véra I remember. I prefer that to the way the living room was when I arrived, all neat and tidy. Oil has leaked all over the counter. I clean up the pools of fat and lumps of grease. As I'm wiping the cloth over the bottom of a cupboard I feel a loose panel. It comes away easily when I press harder. Behind the panel there's a space the size of a vegetable crate cut into the stone wall. It's full of bottles of strong spirits, packets of sugar. I call Véra. She wasn't aware of this alcove either. Does she think perhaps our father was . . . ? She shakes her head, probably not. I agree, I never saw him drinking either.

'And Maman?'

Véra looks thoughtful. I pick up one of the bottles. Quince liqueur. When I go to put it in the bin, she stops me, mimes us drinking it from the bottle. I shake my head but put it back and close the secret hiding place. I turn my attention to the sink – globs of jam floating in brackish water. I have to plunge my arm right in to fish them out.

Véra seems impressed by my system of organising. She looks at me, tugs at her jumper and points to the stairs: she wants me to go up and sort through my clothes.

'I'm giving them all away.'

She insists. I'm conscious of her watching me as I climb the stairs. I can feel the weight of her gaze, it makes even the most trivial gestures seem significant.

My side of the chest of drawers is the same as it was before I left for the US, minus one or two jumpers.

I decide to try on a pair of jeans anyway. Just for fun. My father had mended a hole in them by sticking on a patch with a flowery motif. He did it with a pan of boiling water. The jeans are loose on me. I must be thinner than I used to be. I'm surprised, I've put on weight these past few months. Irvin likes it, which I find both comforting and worrying. I put the jeans in a bag along with the flannel trousers I never wore. Cotton pyjamas, T-shirts, woollen jumpers. I rummage around, feeling more and more that I'm looking for something.

'Where are my skating outfits?' I ask Véra as I come down the stairs carrying several bags.

She hesitates, gestures vaguely with her hand.

'You threw them out?'

She shrugs as she walks back upstairs: apparently, I told her to do what she wanted with them.

There's a saucepan left out on the hob. Spiders teeter along the handle and scuttle away to hide under the furniture.

In the afternoon we go out. To get to the woodland paths you have to walk through the vegetable patch. The raspberry bush is still doubled over after last night's downpour. The carrot tops and radish leaves too. Véra is pleased, we'll have plenty to eat.

'And pasta,' I say.

Véra taps her fingers on her belly. She's trying to cut down on gluten. I glance at her flat stomach, I can see she still exercises regularly.

'All these fads,' I say. 'I'm so fed up with them. When you live in New York it's one thing after another: organic hemp milk, avocado toast, seeds.'

Véra nods slowly in agreement.

The path runs alongside the stream. The ground is red and orange, covered with fallen leaves after the storm. Most of the trees are white oaks. I scoot along in my old boots, crushing slugs underfoot. My father always insisted on buying me boots a size too big, he was convinced my feet were still growing. I've ended up wearing a size smaller than I did then, probably from years of squeezing my feet into high heels.

The vegetation grows denser, we have to duck our heads as we walk. Véra clears the brambles using her secateurs and a stick. Her cheeks flush a dark red. She has rosacea. I try not to think about how unattractive it is. I can barely see her among the trees, she's camouflaged by the brown patchwork jacket she's wearing.

I'm annoyed about my skating things, I don't remember giving her permission to get rid of them. Not that I'd have ever worn them again.

I don't know how I did it, pushing my body to the limit out on the ice like that for so many hours each week, ankles straining to balance on the blades, tendons inflamed, music blasting from speakers.

During the winter we trained in a temporary structure erected on an industrial estate on the outskirts of Périgueux. The rest of the year, we did artistic and rhythmic gymnastics to maintain our fitness. I started quite late, when I was eight. My dream was to make it into the club in Limoges or one of the other cities further north. I used to catch the first bus at six in the morning to go and practise alone on the ice before school. The group sessions were in the evening. After practice I'd wait for the bus in front of the cathedral. I would go inside the cathedral and do my homework by candlelight. There were usually plenty of votive candles already burning but sometimes I'd light them myself. You were supposed to put money in the box but I never did.

We arrive at the pond in the dell. The surface of the water is smooth and black with peat. Down here there's no wind. A figure of a woman carved in stone crouches on one of the rocks in an outcropping near the bank, her face turned towards the water. The château looms above us, curved in on itself like a snail, the tower and the pigeonnier its antennae. We take the shortcut through the limestone rock, along the cluzeaux, natural galleries that were supposedly once used as shelters. The path is quite steep in places. Véra hops and skips to avoid the mud. I'm amazed at her level of energy. I don't talk. I don't want her to notice that I'm out of breath.

The hedges beyond the gate need trimming. The kitchen garden is overgrown. Through the open stable doors I can see stalls, a car, two donkeys, one with strangely cropped ears.

Octave's tall figure appears, wearing a green raincoat. Véra hurries to meet him. I watch them as they hug, they seem to be close. I hang back, taking in Octave's height. He's thirty-five, five years older than I am. He's always been tall but now he seems immense, out of reach. Véra looks so tiny in his arms. He turns to me and says:

'The American! Finally!'

Without waiting for me to respond he starts leading us towards the recently renovated tower. On the way we walk past the pigeonnier. I've never seen it like this before, surrounded by scaffolding and draped in white. Disjointed, recovering from injury.

A damp draught blows from the stairwell. Octave warns us to take care, the walls are thick and the steps are surprisingly narrow. We follow him up the stairs, exchanging platitudes as we climb. He's gleaned a little about me from the press and social media. He tells me he's still working with the University of Limoges as an environmental archaeologist. I have no idea what that involves.

'It's basically studying the way human societies interact with their environment,' he says. 'We look at the historical impact of humans on the environment, the way various living things have responded. Plants and animals, as well as humans.'

He stops and turns to us before adding:

'What we're actually trying to do, of course, is work out what's going on right now.'

The first floor of the tower is used for storing fishing gear. Véra inspects the jars of dried worms, tests the weight of the rods, runs her finger over the blade of an axe that must date from the Middle Ages.

I go on up to the second floor, Octave following on behind me. High ceiling, disused fireplace, pumpkins lined up along one wall. A plastic bat has fallen from a wire hanging from one of the beams. Octave pulls a face, says his daughter wanted to have a party for Halloween, he hasn't had a chance to clear up. He'd tried to make a four-poster bed. I look down at the mattress sitting on top of pallets, a fishing rod planted at each of its corners. I try and imagine him as a father. I ask how old his kid is, doing my best to sound offhand.

'She's five.'

'Is she here with you?'

'She's at her mother's, for the holidays.'

He scrapes his hand over his face as if he's trying to erase something. Looking down at my feet I catch a glimpse of Véra still peering at the jars on the floor below. I can see her through the gaps between the floorboards. I walk over to the window. The glass is cracked, the pond and the statue just visible.

'I've ordered stained glass windows,' Octave says.

I make a joke about the name of the château, Le Pigeon Froid, the cold pigeon. He smiles gently.

'I know, it's not very appealing.'

Véra comes up to join us and we resume our climb. Octave wants to show me the renovations to the battlements. Outside, we look down through the gaps in the parapet from a dizzying height. The tower dates back to the twelfth century. It's one of the most ancient structures in the region. Octave starts explaining about the machicolations, how they were used for defence. I can't help feeling irritated. The explanation is for my benefit, Véra already knows all this. I do too, he ought to realise that. He used to come to our house often enough to borrow books from my father.

I kneel down, feeling dizzy. Cold sunlight on the burnished countryside, the village set out below, buildings scattered like ruins marked out in an archaeological site. Octave says the population has shrunk to the lowest number ever, thirty-three, including the smallholders and the artisans who work at the Hermès plant and the knife factory in Nontron. The school has closed down. But the fromagerie is still there, supplying cheese to gourmet restaurants as far away as Sarlat and Rocamadour.

There's a clear view of the pigeonnier across the courtyard. Looking at it from here you wouldn't know there had ever been a fire there. It happened a hundred years ago. No one knows how it started. My father had plenty of theories, he was always talking about it. I never went inside. The door was always jammed shut. I still think about the birds trapped in there, unable to fly out. I imagine macabre scenarios – are there skeletons in there still? Is the floor carpeted with the incinerated remains of the birds that perished?

In the gathering darkness of late afternoon, the pond has melted away. Only the statue is visible, her neck twisted by a trick of perspective. No longer gazing at the water, she seems to be trying to catch our eye.

Véra brushes my sleeve lightly to let me know she wants us to leave. On the way back, as we pass the stable, I look more closely at the donkey with cropped ears and realise it's a llama.

In the evening I go up to the bedroom before Véra and do some work in bed. My emails have been mounting up. The internet connection keeps dropping out. There are six of us working on the screenplay. I haven't met any of the others in person. When we first embarked on the project I suggested we get together for a meal and a work session. Everyone agreed it was a great idea. Six months later I'd still had no response to my suggested dates and had to accept that we'd be doing all our communicating online.

The novel we're adapting is structured in two alternating parts. One is an autobiographical account of

Perec's memories of his childhood during the Second World War. The other describes a fictional island dedicated entirely to sport, which gradually emerges as a metaphor for the concentration camp in which his parents perished.

I read over the ideas I drafted before leaving New York. They seem less interesting now. Moonlight filters through the window, streaking the ceiling. I savour the silence. I still haven't adjusted to the sirens in New York. A spider twitches above my head. I could reach out and touch it. I never see any in New York. I watch it carefully, in case it decides to weave its web right next to my face. The spiders are the reason Véra has the bottom bunk. When we were growing up, we used to get into bed together more and more frequently as tension mounted between our parents.

'Don't worry, Véra,' I'd say over and over again, cradling her in my arms. 'Everything will be all right, you'll see.' I was never really sure which of us I was trying to reassure, Véra or myself.

I find it hard to remember that we were inseparable once upon a time. We were both timid. Both fearful of social interactions. We didn't squabble. We were bound together by our shared language of silence and cries.

I can't really remember how her silence began. Véra was six. We were eating, my father, Véra and I. My father asked her a question and she didn't reply. We thought it must be a tantrum of sorts. My mother wasn't there, she was working. My father grew impatient. Véra started breathing hard, her face contorted. Strange sounds came out of her mouth, somewhere between groaning and gurgling. Choking. She never uttered another word after that. I don't know what it feels like to her, but I do know that since I had the epidural, I've understood how frightening it can be to have the impression you can't breathe. You think you're dying, you start to black out.

Véra never complained of any physical or emotional trauma. The doctors said the most likely cause was a ruptured aneurism, rare as that is in children. The speech therapists explained the situation to us, making it clear that aphasia can take many forms. Every case is different. Some individuals can understand the written word but are unable to speak coherently, others confuse words, saying things like 'ballot' instead of 'rabbit', or they fail to realise that what they are saying makes no sense at all: 'I'm cold' for example when they mean 'I love you'. For the family, the advice is always the same: be patient, ask simple questions that can be answered with a nod or a shake of the head, speak slowly, don't finish sentences for the person suffering from aphasia, and don't correct their mistakes. But what about with a child? Where do you draw the line between a disability and a normal process of learning? My father asked if there could be a psychological cause. Probably not. I think this uncertainty was the most painful aspect of it for me. I was never able to let go of the suspicion that Véra had intentionally denied me access to her inner world.

8 NOVEMBER

I wake up with the sun, my head freezing in this unheated room. I stay huddled under the covers. For a moment, I think I hear my father's footsteps. I open my eyes and lean over the guardrail. Véra's not in her bed, her blankets are rumpled. With a start I notice the time, eleven o'clock. I climb down the ladder, shivering at the touch of the metal rungs.

Downstairs on the table I find a clean plate, a jar of honey and some sourdough bread wrapped in a cloth. Véra's shoes are no longer by the door. I burn my index finger trying to light the gas. I'm out of the habit of doing this. I run my finger under cold water for several minutes. The cheese smell in the room is getting stronger.

I go back upstairs to the bedroom and close the door. I wish Véra had warned me that she'd be out. I can't write if I think I might be interrupted at any moment. Even with Irvin, I ask him to tell me his plans for the day. I move the desk over to face the window. The chestnut tree fans out, its five-fingered branches coated with a sheen of blue-green moss. The tree is bare except for the occasional solitary green leaf clinging to the tip of a branch. I wonder about the colour of these leaves; is the tree putting on new growth or are they the most resilient of the old leaves?

We're working on episode four. A key event occurs. The athlete at the centre of the plot has just won a race, not realising that this means certain death. The challenge for us is to generate emotions without pathos. I'm writing in English. The French version will be subtitled by professional translators.

I give up on typing, my burnt finger is bothering me. I decide to watch an interview with Perec instead. He's talking about his writing process, looking off to the side, smiling. He comes across as uncomplicated. The interviewer asks him to list twenty-five things he'd like to do before he dies. Perec doesn't know at this point that within three months he will be dead. I pause the video. He's just said he thinks he lacks imagination, he has to search for inspiration. I scribble a few words half-heartedly, make myself some more coffee.

Later, I put on a coat and go outside. Sitting down on a rock against the wall, I munch on some nuts and cheese. The sun is high in the sky. I turn my face upwards to warm it in the sunlight.

Near the door, a line of ants stretches along the wall to a small gap in the chimney breast. They're carrying seeds. I stare at them as I eat, fascinated, wondering how to get rid of them.

After a while I go back inside and wash the dishes left in the sink. Then I settle down to work at the table in the living room and wait for Véra to come home.

Halfway through the afternoon I decide to message her.

```
Dear Véra.
```
Too formal.
```
Hi Véra.
```
```
Véra.
```

I put my phone down. Some scriptwriter, I think to myself, you can't even write to your own sister.

I go back to my script. Realising I'm reading the same sequence over again for the third time, I close my laptop and go out to look for her.

The path we cleared for ourselves last time is easy to find. I follow the animal tracks through the undergrowth feeling less nervous than I did yesterday. The earth is starting to dry out. In my trainers, I can move faster. I take the shortcut past the cluzeaux. I climb, grabbing at overhanging branches to keep myself from falling into the ravine. It's exhausting. I hadn't realised I was so out of shape. I haven't been exercising lately, I stopped because of the nausea. My route takes me through one of the tunnels past a niche in the wall where hunters have left a stash of saucisson and Coca-Cola.

I arrive at the edge of the field where Octave's grandmother is buried. She lost her husband during the war and it was her wish to be buried here near the château. The tomb faces her private chapel, dwarfing the surrounding bushes. Shrubs don't grow very tall in these parts, the soil is thin and pitted with stones. Life lived out beneath a veil of rocks.

The pond is on the other side of the field.

As I thought, Véra is down by the water. I didn't spot her at first because of her coat. She swings her arms as she walks. She stops, leans over the surface of the water, starts walking again with that peculiar gait, hood pulled up like a snout over her head.

I retrace my steps, go back to the house, locking the door behind me.

I hear her crossing the courtyard and look through the spy hole. She looks so small that I think she's still several metres away, but she's already at the door. I open it hastily. She asks me if I had a productive day. I remark curtly that she could have told me she was going to be out. She looks surprised, drums her fingers on an imaginary keyboard, points at my phone. I shake my head, I didn't get any messages. While she's taking off her coat I double check and feel slightly ashamed; she did send me a message, just before I went out. I'd left my phone on silent. She hands me a pot of jam, from Octave.

'He makes jam?'

Big lumps of fruit are pressed up against the glass, light brown and sloppy, like wet sand. A mixture of strawberries and figs perhaps? I struggle with the lid, picturing Véra and Octave together in the château. She looks down at the ants. She hadn't seen them before either. We both wonder what we can do to get rid of them. Can we do it without killing them? She takes a lemon, cuts it in half, squeezes it over the column of ants, puts the squeezed lemon in the corner of the doorway. I ask her where she learnt to do that.

She pulls herself upright and shows me her phone again.

Papa taught me.

She gives me that look I find so unnerving, the one that says 'obviously'.

At our feet, there's a scene of chaos in miniature. The ants have started jumping around on contact with the acid, they drop their loads, crash into one another, spread out across the tiles like links broken from a chain.

I don't know how my father and Véra managed on a day-to-day level, how they learnt to communicate with one another without me. I don't ask her, I don't want to talk about the fact that I left.

My father would phone me from time to time to tell me how Véra was doing. Our conversations were almost exclusively about her. I never talked about myself. I could tell he was afraid of grilling me, but he stayed on the line. He'd tell me all about the caves, the numbers of people who came to visit them, the thirteen-degree difference in temperature between the interior of the caves and the air outside that was constantly battered by winds from the Atlantic and the Auvergne. And then, his voice wavering as if with regret, he'd ask how I was. Fine, I'd say. I could tell it made him sad that I wasn't more forthcoming. I liked the fact that he felt sad but I did feel guilty. I clammed up even more, he called less and less frequently until in the end I stopped answering when he rang. For several years our communication was limited to three or four emails a year, on birthdays and Christmas. My father stopped telling me about himself and gave me no more news of Véra. He talked about the house instead: 'everything is fine with the house', 'the house is fine', 'the living room has a bit of damp', 'I've cut back the ivy on the roof', 'we've got some carrots in the garden', 'we found wild boar tracks outside the door'. I think the references to 'we' stopped me from answering too. At the end of the message he'd always ask me how I was doing and I'd write back and say: 'Everything is fine.' I had no direct contact with Véra. The last time I spoke to my father was on the phone. He rang while I was on a video call for work. I answered, surprised that he was calling. He wanted to know how I was feeling. I gave my usual answer. I was angry with myself for having given in and taken the call, but I'd met Irvin, I was in love, I couldn't keep it to myself. We talked about Irvin, about how well I'd been doing at work. He was quiet for a few moments before saying gently:

'That's good to know.'

He said I was lucky to be having all these experiences. He was very happy for me. Then he called me by my name. 'I'm happy for you, Agathe.' He'd never done that before. I always felt like he was talking to someone else. At home, we were always 'the girls', even when he was only talking to me. And then, for the first time, I told him the truth. I couldn't go on lying to him anymore. I told him how hard it was, New York, the people, the job.

'I'm sorry,' was all he said.

'You don't need to worry,' I stammered.

He hung up. I didn't go back to the meeting, I cried for ten minutes. Three months later Véra got in touch with me. She sent me a text. Her number wasn't in my contacts. Papa's dead. It seemed so ridiculous that I immediately replied: Who is this? It dawned on me instantly that it had to be her. Who else could it be?

Octave? He would never have used those words. I also realised that aside from my father, no one ever wrote to me in French.

We go back to sorting things downstairs together. The armoire is full of LPs, bolts of fabric, Tibetan prayer flags, hooks, saucers, candles, small bits and pieces of metal whose usefulness is a mystery to me. I let Véra deal with them while I get to work on the books in the fireplace. Classics, their pages falling out. I waste time flipping through them. Books about the caves. Science fiction, Jules Verne. Georges Simenon's *The Cat*, cloth-bound, the cover devoid of lettering. I run my fingers lightly over it. Maps of the area, children's books. I place them in a pile beside me, then realise that all I'm doing is moving them from one place to another.

We could listen to music to fill our silences. I don't suggest it. I don't listen to much music, and never for pleasure. I sometimes have it playing softly through headphones when I'm writing; I find it tiring but it forces me to concentrate. I'm left feeling exhausted but with the sensation of having accomplished something.

In the boxes beside the fireplace I find bric-a-brac from Eastern Europe – Russian dolls and glassware that my mother collected. She was the main earner in our family. My father supplemented our income with the money he earned during the tourist season working as a guide in the caves. He'd used up his inheritance on renovating this house. It took up all his free time too.

I was nine when she left. For the first few years we saw her once a year in the period between Christmas and New Year. She would come back from London for several days and stay in a hotel. The one time that Véra and I went to see her, we shared a single bed in her new partner's children's room. They were the same age as we were. I was already speaking for Véra by then. His family got our names wrong every time for a whole week. We refused to go back there again. She was pregnant at my father's funeral.

Time has made it easier to remember my mother. She is preserved in amber. Even when she was with us, she was absent. She used to work in the bedroom, on the bed, surrounded by hot-water bottles which my father would refill for her. We weren't allowed to disturb her. Whenever she came down to make herself some tea, she'd brush her fingers distractedly through my hair. Some part of her was reaching for elsewhere; she moved haltingly, as if there was a delay between thought and movement. I can see my father, placing his hand lightly on her hip when they passed one another. Whenever they argued, I would always try and keep Véra occupied. They usually quarrelled in their bedroom. Sometimes they'd go for days without speaking at all. Véra and I would make ourselves scarce. We weren't trying to avoid them, but on the days when they weren't speaking, if one of us happened to catch another's eye, we'd all four turn our gaze quietly inwards.

One day, when she came home from a work trip, my mother threw her arms round my father. He flinched. She was in tears. I can hear him saying to her that it's normal. Or not normal. That she's not normal. Looking back, I think what he meant was that she was upset, she wasn't in her normal frame of mind. I wanted to comfort her afterwards. She shut herself in her bedroom. When I opened the door she pushed me away, her hand flat against my chest. I froze, her fingers were like ice. I heard my father calling us:

'Girls!'

He took me out for a walk with Véra, just as he always did. He bent down over the surface of the pond, the water inky black. It was nightfall, moonlight. We crouched down. My father took a stick and ruffled the surface of the water.

'Why is the moon not reflected in this pond?' he asked. 'It's shining brightly in the sky.'

'Because of the peat,' I said, feeling proud of myself.

My father smiled at me then looked at Véra who was staring wide-eyed. He was silent for a moment and then, adopting his story-telling voice, he said:

'There was a time when the moon was reflected in our pond just as it is in water all over the world. One evening, transfixed by the beauty of her own image, the moon plunged into the water. The darkness thickened, the night sky was shrouded in a dense black pall. From inside the château, one woman had witnessed the whole scene. Thinking the moon was drowning, she dived in to rescue her. The following morning the woman was found by her true love at the water's edge. Her mouth and eyes were waterlogged and bloated. Inside her belly, something was gleaming. Her lover parted her insides to reveal what he thought at first was an egg. But it was too heavy to be an egg. It was a stone. Wracked by grief, he took the stone and placed it in the pigeonnier, hoping it would spur the birds to lay more eggs and cause everything in the surrounding lands to flourish in memory of his lost love.'

Eight o'clock already. Véra's hungry. She won't let me help her. I don't insist, I never cook, Irvin does it all, or else I order something in. She's deep in concentration. The knife slices through the cabbage, her hands hover above the stove. She lights the gas, sprinkles salt and pepper instinctively, opens a tube of tomato concentrate, squeezes out a spoonful, wipes the counter clean. Her fingertips are red, purple, they leave marks on everything she touches. She chuckles silently to herself as she works. I watch her intently. She's become so adept in the kitchen. It would take me an hour to do what she's just done. She moves confidently, making full use of the space, not bumping into anything, her stance is firm, every gesture preceded by a glance. First the eyes, then an inclination of the head, then hips, hands, legs and feet. She's sautéed the cabbage, now she's making pastry, stretching it by hand until it's almost transparent. I find it fascinating to watch her taking so much time to prepare a meal that will vanish in an instant. Still fully focused, she brushes the pastry with olive oil. The pastry soaks it up, she's used almost the whole bottle. I pour myself a glass of water. Since my return, she's taken to looking at me and smiling every time our paths cross. To get my attention. I pretend I haven't seen. I never know what to say.

I go back to sorting through books. There's a whole pile of cookery books. I amuse myself skimming through recipes, glancing at the photographs that go with them. Old smells, sour. Wobbly aspics, tripe, omelettes. Clear soups. An instruction manual with recipes for the 'Super Cocotte', the first pressure cooker from the 1950s. Pictures above the recipes of young chefs, posing proudly. Where are they now, I wonder. And their creations? Do people still use their recipes? Véra looks over my shoulder, she's intrigued by the tripe recipe, wants to try it. I don't eat tripe. Neither does she. But she's curious.

On the next page there's a recipe for blanquette de veau with mushrooms. We used to have it at school, served with broccoli you could crush with a fork. That dining hall, a medieval building with high windows. Condensation that made our hair curl. We had to wear a bright yellow armband with the school badge on it. We looked like battery chickens kept alive on a diet of idiot fodder. Véra's classroom was next to the refectory, across the courtyard from mine. She'd stand by the door at lunchtime and wait for me, craning her neck towards the queue to make sure I hadn't abandoned her. We had to get there early to find two seats together.

Rumours about Véra not talking began to circulate. One Sunday in November, the girl sitting next to me at lunch – her name was Margaux, I knew her by sight, she was in the year between Véra and me – leant across my plate and asked Véra her name. I answered for her. Margaux said she knew perfectly well what it was, she was just wondering if my sister realised her name sounded just like the word for a male pig. I asked her to please not say things like that. Véra was eating her blanquette, strands of hair trailing in the sauce. Margaux gave her a pointed look. She fiddled with the mushrooms on her own plate, a spongy mass with pink spots. Mushrooms were a bit like tongues, she announced, maybe something intelligible would come out of Véra's mouth now, she'd been stuffing enough of them into her face. Véra looked up, cheeks puffed out. She turned to look straight at Margaux, leant across over my plate and spat as hard as she could. Out came a pale slimy mass that looked like mashed slugs. Then she stuck out her tongue, scraped it between her teeth and spat directly at Margaux, who sat there, stock-still, drool dripping from her hair. The whole dining hall fell silent. Margaux looked at Véra and then at me, opening and closing her mouth without uttering a sound. I'd been splattered too. I picked up the bits of mushroom that had landed on my spoon and put them in my mouth, acting as if they were delicious. Margaux finally said something about us both being nuts and got up to leave the table. I waited until she'd gone before wiping my face.

Véra carried on eating, dipping bits of bread into her yoghurt as if she was eating a boiled egg. Her face portrayed no emotion but on close inspection you could see that her hands and chin were trembling.

Margaux came back flanked by the housemistress. Normally I had faith in the housemistress, but seeing her stern expression I lost all confidence. She asked me to give my version of events. Then she looked the three of us up and down and announced that Margaux, Véra and I would all have detention for the next few days.

After school I went to see her to tell her again that Véra and I had done nothing wrong. The housemistress gave me a knowing look. Disagreements could arise, she said, there was no harm in that. But not owning up when you were in the wrong was a serious matter. She looked at me long and hard and said there was nothing worse than telling lies.

The pastry is light and crispy, from all that olive oil she brushed it with. Véra arranges the cheese on a plate and starts on the jar of Octave's jam that she's managed to open with the point of a knife. She cuts a slice of cheese and places it on some bread. Then she licks the knife and sticks it back into the jar of jam. I point out that this will make the jam spoil more quickly. She laughs and says we'll have eaten it all before then. I decide this is a good opportunity to mention the cheese sitting in the birdcage. It's giving off a smell that turns my stomach.

```
It needs to age.
```

Then she winks at me and adds:

Needs to be aged.

I press the point and say something about invisible spores multiplying, the cheese developing a layer of green mould. She screws the lid back on the jam jar and sighs as she types:

Sense of humour. Please.

After dinner we clear the table and bring the lamp closer. Véra spreads out a set of cutlery that our mother brought back from her travels. She arranges the pieces in order of size and wipes them with a cloth while I pick up the packaging ready to put the whole set in the pile of things to dispose of. But she takes the packaging from my hand, rewraps each piece of cutlery and sets it to one side. I'm sure she doesn't actually want to keep them.

I'm reluctant to leave Véra on her own in the living room so I carry on sorting rather half-heartedly through the books. Freed of much of the clutter, the fireplace looks almost like another room, one that's black with soot. I turn to the stack of books. Classic editions piled up on top of cartoon albums. I once had a whole set of Philemon albums that my father gave me – the adventures of a young boy in a bucolic, pre-industrial world. With his father and Anatole the donkey as his companions, Philemon sets out on his travels and discovers a parallel world of islands in the shape of letters that make up the words Atlantic Ocean. Wintry, wind-blown landscapes, bare trees. I used to embark on every album hoping it would transport me to a sunnier world. It never did but there was always something comforting about the familiar autumnal setting. Further down in the pile, Raymond Briggs, *The Snowman*, a tale of loss and transformation. A memory comes back to me of a cartoon I often used to watch with Véra. A boy with a round face. Nighttime, just before Christmas. The boy longs for a present, an electric train he's seen in a shop window. The family can't afford to buy it but the boy lies awake night after night thinking about the train. In the end the shopkeeper gives it to him. Or maybe his father does? The film ends with the train flying away, the boy in the driver's seat. Perhaps he died.

The entire collection is book-ended by a pair of crates filled with our school things. My exercise books filled with compositions, geometry, diagrams of internal organs. Underneath them, Véra's notebooks. Inside, they're a mess. She struggled to keep up with the mainstream classes and had to repeat several years. The year she turned eight she signed all her homework diaries as 'Mandarine'. I kept telling her it wasn't a real name, least of all hers, but she'd get so angry that I gave up. I remember thinking it was a prettier name than Véra anyway.

Back then the doctors were optimistic about the possibility of her learning to talk again. They encouraged us to stimulate her and not talk down to her.

After my mother left, my father had to take on more work out of season. He had to travel further too, sometimes to places two hours away like the Gouffre de Padirac, the one at Proumeyssac or the caves at Lascaux. He'd leave before eight in the morning and not get home until ten o'clock at night. He used to make soup for us ahead of time using vegetables from the garden. I ended up dumping it out in the forest because Véra only ever wanted to have pasta. I decided I'd have to get my vitamins from school meals. To make life easier, I drew up a list of different pasta sauces and asked her to indicate with a nod which ones she liked. That was how I planned our evening meals – tortellini with gorgonzola, parmesan, mozzarella, Octave's grandmother's bolognaise sauce.

When my father came home, he'd go upstairs and change. We were supposed to be in bed asleep. He'd open our door slowly and place the back of his hand on our foreheads, as if to check our temperature. I'd lie awake, pretending to be asleep, until I felt his touch. Only then could I fall asleep. The day came when I was old enough to wait up. Véra would be in bed and I'd sit on the couch reading. I used to leave a place setting at the table for my father, with the best silverware. As time went by he'd come home more and more tired. Almost imperceptibly he started moving more slowly, taking longer each evening to come back down from the bedroom to eat.

One evening, I must have been twelve or thirteen at the time, he took so long I began to worry. I went upstairs. The door was open. My father was stretched out on the bed wearing his heavy wool jumper, his feet on the floor, one hand pressed to his eyes. I drew closer. I could see the veins throbbing in his neck. He said he wasn't going to have anything to eat that evening. It seemed to me as if an alien creature had wormed its way into his body. He raised his other hand from his chest, I tried to imagine his heart beating inside that powerful frame. I can still feel his great hands taking hold of me as he said: don't be afraid, I'm here. But what I remember most of that moment is the slight pain in my chest, a small, barely perceptible sensation.

Sometimes, Véra had to come with me to the ice rink after school. She'd wait for me in the stands. I could see her in outline, bundled up in her down jacket with its fake fur hood, her presence weighing on me. Afterwards we'd wait for the bus in front of the cathedral opposite the municipal car park. Our bus didn't run very often, the wait was forty minutes. If the cathedral was open, we'd go inside and pull faces at our reflections in the stained-glass windows or play at being statues of sleeping saints. Lying there so stiff, they reminded me of myself lying rigidly in our little bed at night, the warmth of Véra's body, my eyes closed onto my own private space.

The day Véra spat at Margaux, someone was setting up a nativity scene with resin figurines in the cathedral hall. Véra planted herself directly in front of the man working on the nativity scene, her arms puffed out in her padded jacket. The man was sticking the manes on the donkey and the ox before applying a coat of varnish. The crib was still empty except for a few chickens. The smell of alcohol mingled with incense was making me feel dizzy. Candles sputtered, making a sound like the crackling of insects frying. I went back outside to wait for the bus.

When it arrived I asked the driver to wait while I ran back inside to get Véra. We were the only passengers. She was standing with her nose practically glued to the ox. The varnish on the figurines had dried, looking almost as if it had frozen. The craftsman had started arranging the figurines – Mary and Joseph at either end, the donkey and ox close to the cradle. Jesus was propped up with legs crossed, hands clasped together in prayer. He was bigger than the other figures. The thought occurred to me that he looked like a baby cuckoo waiting to be fed. I clasped Véra by the shoulder. I felt a slight resistance at first but then she followed me, just far enough away to prevent me from holding her hand.

In the bus, squeezed between our bags, we were jolted around by the bumps in the road. Véra had the window seat, I usually let her have it. That evening, she was gazing down at the ground, her scarf wrapped tightly around her cheeks, her lips bright red. Her nose was running. I could see she was cold. I pressed my hand to her mitten and said:

'I'll always be there for you.'

Half past ten. Véra scans the room – piles of books, bin bags. She looks pleased, concludes happily that we'll have more time for ourselves. She asks me what I'm planning to do tomorrow. I'm not on holiday, I say. She raises an eyebrow, looks askance at me: neither is she. She was simply being polite. She's going mushroom picking.

I take a picture book up to bed with me, Claude Ponti's *L'arbre sans fin*, The Tree Without End. I still remember the scene where the little creature in the story, in mourning for her grandmother, finds herself a prisoner on the planet of a million mirrors. Every mirror gives a slightly different image, the only way to escape is by finding the mirror that reflects us as we really are. I still wonder how the little creature managed to find the right one so easily.

9 NOVEMBER

Véra crouches beside the pond washing her hands, sleeves rolled up to the elbows, her basket filled with mushrooms. I felt obliged to come with her. My writing problems are nothing to do with her, I shouldn't inflict my insecurities on her. But I don't know my mushrooms like she does: I keep thinking I've spotted one but it usually turns out to be a stone or a branch or the skeleton of a rodent, so I've gone back to picking berries. I head towards the bushes, there are rosehips everywhere, we'll be able to make rosehip tea. I come to a stand of oak trees. A massive tree stump sits proudly in their midst, rising to shoulder height, its circumference so vast that Véra and I together wouldn't be able to encircle it with our arms.

A moment later I hear a rustling of leaves in the undergrowth. A wild boar. There in front of me. Massive, hairy, humped back, almost the size of the tree stump. He turns his head from side to side, snout creased and twitching. He moves closer. I crouch behind the tree stump, almost losing sight of him. An animal smell, sour and penetrating, cuts through the odour of damp wood. I feel a jolt. Then another. I tell myself a lone boar has no reason to attack a person. He'd have turned around if he'd seen me. More jolts, harder, more frequent. As if the animal were venting a deep-seated rage.

I hear a new sound, the trampling of undergrowth. The boar backs up, his head moving from side to side again. Our eyes meet. I start, in horror. A hole, where one eye should be. An open wound, puss congealed around the eyelid. The boar turns his head and finally, with his one good eye, he sees me. I can't take my eyes off the wound, the boar scraping it against the tree stump, grunting, neck and shoulders streaked with blood. I hear footsteps approaching. The boar staggers off into the undergrowth at a stately, almost dignified pace.

A man appears, rifle slung across his chest. Orange high-visibility jacket. He must be about my age, loose-limbed, curls escaping from beneath his cap. Panicked at the sight of me there right in the middle of the hunt. He's out of breath. Asks why I didn't heed the signs posted on the outskirts of the forest. I explain that our house is inside the forest, I had no way of knowing. My sister is out there too, in a jacket that's hard to see, the other hunters should be told. He says something into his headset. A trumpet sounds in the distance. He glances at the rosehips in my basket, asks if I'm authorised to pick them. I laugh.

'Who cares?' I say. 'There are tons of them, rotting on the bushes.'

He wants to know where I'm from.

'I was born here.'

He says he's never seen me before.

'I've never seen you either.'

His tone grows harsher. He says I'm scaring away the boars, I have to leave. I realise I'm sweating. To my great relief Véra appears, her basket spilling over with mushrooms, her hands full too. She looks at the hunter, her face expressionless. I walk over to her. Standing close to her I can sense a vibration, as if all her muscles are tensed beneath the layers of clothing. The hunter looks us up and down. He points off to one side, says we'll be safe in that direction. Then he turns his back on us and walks away, grumbling about us not wearing high-vis clothing.

We go back up to the field where the tombs are. Whisps of smoke hover above the rocky ground, held in place by the unseasonably warm air. Véra stops to type something on her phone. I carry on walking thinking she is probably doing it on purpose, a way of pausing discreetly to give me time to catch my breath. She runs up to me waving her phone:

Smoke: Papa used to say it was the rabbits making their coffee!

I've never heard that one. I force a smile. I find it hurtful when she talks about her life with my father without me.

From up here, the forest looks flattened, rolled out like a swathe of foam matting. You're less aware of the contours, the rivers deep in the valleys. The wind picks up. It occurs to me that this was all steppe once, before the forests, in prehistoric times. Back then, the climate here was more like it is in Scandinavia today. Erosion.

This landscape raked by wind and water, unhindered by obstacles of any kind.

At this time of year in New York, the wind is like ice. It sweeps through the streets, crashing into buildings, spinning in frantic circles and slamming against the windows. In recent weeks I've walked for hours on end in this wind. Irvin leaves for work in the morning. Usually I revel in the solitude, it gives me a chance to work. But I'd started to hate it. I couldn't sit at that table by the window anymore. As soon as he left, I'd go out. I didn't have a plan. I'd listen to my footsteps on the pavement, feel my blood pulsing beneath my hat, watch my breath. It kept me calm until the moment later in the day when I'd lay my head on Irvin's chest and feel reassured by the sound of his heartbeat. He didn't share my doubts, I couldn't make him understand. Nor was I sure I wanted an abortion. Véra had just asked me to come and join her. I'd decided for the moment to say no to her because of the pregnancy, whatever the outcome.

'Girls!'

The sound of my father's voice echoing through the limestone tunnel, amplified by the speakers linked to his microphone. Sheepishly we catch up with the group. Our palms are moist with spit. We're six and seven years old, it's the autumn holiday. We're walking deep in the Padirac caverns, three hundred metres below the surface, alongside a stream. Outside it's raining hard. The cave entrance acts as a funnel, channelling the rain as it falls from the sky. Down here the temperature remains constant, the humidity levels stable. The only movement of air comes from our breath. My father is talking about sedimentation, concretion, calcium deposits. He shines his torch, pointing out examples, his words transforming the rock formations into flowers, fur, musical instruments, the limestone columns into statues, people turned to stone drop by drop.

We're under strict instructions not to touch anything. The limestone is alive. I take my father's instructions to heart. It's my job to restrain Véra. He explains how sebum in our skin prevents water from clinging to the rock and making it grow. The thought that my touch alone can kill a mineral structure thousands of years old terrifies me. I'm fascinated too by the idea that these shapes are formed by water, just as every cell in my body is made up of water and minerals.

Véra and I are trying to make some stalagmites of our own. It was my idea. We could spit into our hands, mix our saliva together and smear it at the base of a cave wall. Then we'd watch to see if the water in the cave would make it grow. But we can't agree on who's going to spit into whose hand, so we decide to spit on the ground. We can't stop giggling. Our father tells us to behave.

He herds the group into a boat, my sister and I at the front. He rows slowly, talking about the stream becoming a river, flowing for thirty kilometres with no source of water other than the rain that seeps through from the ground above. It brings impurities that feed the rare life forms capable of surviving here – snails, minuscule shrimps. Slowly his voice takes on a different tenor as he tells how the concretions are born from the water's jealousy of the mountains that point skyward and cause so much excitement among humans. To compete with those peaks, he says, the most determined drops of water have found a way to be like the mountains, here, underground where darkness and stillness prevail.

I look down at my hands. I could turn into a statue too. If I'm envious I'll be turned to stone, I'll be like a block of ice. But if it's hot, I'll melt. I need it to be cold so I can feel stronger, so I can stand upright.

How's Irvin?

Véra stuffs her phone into her pocket and starts walking again. Having her ask me about him like that comes as a surprise. I've never actually talked to her about Irvin. I give her some factual information, where we live, how long we've been together, what he does for a living. Nothing too personal. Underneath, I'm trying to think of fictional characters I could mention that would help me to describe him. I realise I have no idea about my sister's tastes in books, film, television. I can't remember a time when she wasn't there, but I have no memories of being an adult with her, except for our father's funeral. Everything ends with me leaving for the US when she was twelve years old. The day she gave me that look that said: you lied to me.

She adjusts her hood. Her bracelets jangle. Who is she wearing them for, I wonder. Does she wear them even when she's alone? I've never known her to be in a relationship. I want to know if she's in love, if she's loved, but I don't know how to talk about love. All I can bring myself to ask is:

'Don't you get bored here in Périgueux?'

She laughs. Not at all, quite the opposite. She wishes she had more time to spend on keeping fit and being with her friends.

'She has friends?' I say under my breath, thinking out loud. I hope she hasn't heard, I wish I hadn't referred to her as 'she'. But to my relief she doesn't seem to have taken offence.

`Personally, I can't love someone unless I admire them,` she informs me conclusively. I can't read the expression on her face.

We take a detour through the village, Véra wants to go back to the cheese shop. She picks out a few small rounds of sheep's cheese, not too soft. I pay, I'm the big sister.

Most of the shutters are closed. Outside the church I notice the recesses at the base of the wall. A sign explains that these are sarcophagi of children who died in the womb or who didn't live long enough to be baptised. The sign wasn't there when I lived here. Mist obscures the Pigeon Froid up on the hill. I think again of what Octave said about how the villages have suffered. The shortage of doctors. The street is deserted, there's no traffic. We walk in single file along the narrow pavement, Véra striding ahead while I lag slowly behind.

Véra, the village.

The images don't fit together. I look up at the shutters, the doors. The vision of Véra swims beneath my eyelids, a mote that only tears can wash away.

We put the mushrooms down in front of the hearth. Véra stands with her back to me. I have to check her for ticks. She's stripped to her underwear, cotton bra, no underwiring, full coverage. She turns to face me. Her breasts point upwards, her body strong, athletic. It's unsettling. My little sister, in a woman's body, more generously proportioned than mine. I do my best to look away, examine her in a hurry. I don't wear a bra. I find it oppressive. Before I met Irvin I allowed my lovers to believe I went braless for their benefit. I didn't want to disappoint them. And besides, I'd had to squeeze my body into corsets the whole time I was training.

The costumes we wore revealed every bulge. As adolescents, we went one of two ways. There were the girls who weren't afraid of men, and the others, like me, who regarded our newly developed curves as shameful. I was sixteen when I had my first period, I'd already moved to the US.

Véra disappears into the shower and I go and wait in the living room.

The ants are still there. They skirt around the lemon, avoiding it, all moving at the same speed. Occasionally one of them stops and rears up, still carrying its load of seeds, turning its head from side to side while its fellow ants butt up against it. A traffic jam forms but the column quickly starts moving again. What is it they find so interesting here? I wonder where the seeds are coming from. Odd that I haven't thought about this before. Looking at them closely I can see they're not all seeds. Translucent specks. Grains of sand. A twig like a roof beam. Body parts, an insect's leg. One of the ants is carrying a dragonfly wing; with its helmet-like head, it looks a bit like a pilot.

I apply some more lemon juice, a little further away from them this time, hoping to create a route that steers them away from me.

A fine stream of ashes falls down the chimney followed by a flurry of feathers. Probably from a birds' nest. The house feels damp after the storm. I need to make sure the boiler is working. There's a door under the stairs outside the front door that leads to where it's housed. I pick up a stick out of habit and use it to push aside the brambles. The boiler is making a soft rumbling sound. I scan the wooden shelves my father built all around it. A can of petrol, cycling helmets, gardening tools. The floor strewn with animal droppings. A dormouse probably.

Back inside the house I announce to Véra that we're almost out of heating oil.

'We ought to light a fire,' I add. 'But I think there might be birds nesting in the chimney.'

Véra nods, shivering, her hair wet from the shower.

I go into the bathroom and lock the door. Blood pulsing through my veins in the hollow of my breastbone. I don't wear makeup when I'm here. My eyes are less puffy than usual, I think I look healthier. I hear shots coming from the far end of the garden, hunting rifles. My heart starts racing. The same happens when I hear sirens in

Manhattan. I heard them all the time in my first apartment there. I lived on my own, in a run-down building on the Lower East Side. People all around me, framed in windows, rushing frantically about or frozen in position, leaning out, cigarette in hand, coils of smoke drifting upwards like dreams evaporating. Rats running along the pipes up to the rooftops where pigeons nest, defying the spikes placed to keep them away.

My closest neighbours had a picture window with no curtains. Cables and an air vent were all that separated us. I could see their bed with its cinder-grey covers. They made no effort to hide their lovemaking. Their heads were hidden against the wall but I could see shoulders and hips moving, I was sure I could hear the rustle of sheets. I felt embarrassed. Then sad. I understood later that they put themselves on display like that because in their eyes I didn't exist. After that, I regarded them with indifference.

I started seeing men. I made no effort to get to know them. I'd drop them without explanation. I ghosted them, became a phantom, a figment of their imagination.

I grew tired of it in the end. Then for three years, I saw no one and spent my time writing film scripts.

I met Irvin on 14 November, Pickle Day, the Jewish festival of pickled cucumbers. His consulting rooms were a few streets away. He was on a break. There was a festive atmosphere. He saw me and came over to give me a gherkin he'd just bought. He said I'd probably find it too salty. Irvin knew nothing about the film world. And from the moment I experienced the sensation of his skin against mine all my own hard-won knowledge began to seem trivial.

I talked to him about it as soon as I found out. I'd assumed my period was late because I was stressed. He turned off the burner under the pasta, walked over to me and placed his hand lightly on my stomach. The way he did it annoyed me. I'd be magnificent with a big belly, he said. I retorted that my stomach was fat and bloated every month before my period. I couldn't stand it. He took his hand away, looked at me full on. Then he wrapped his arms around me. I buried my head in his shoulder to make it seem like I was overjoyed. And to hide my fear. I had only myself to blame. In the heat of the moment I'd asked him to come inside me. I think some part of me wanted to be pregnant, to know what it was like. But a little voice inside kept goading me, reminding me that no one gets pregnant just for the experience.

The dim lighting makes the space in the room around Véra seem smaller. She's taken down some of the posters from the wall to draw on them with my father's charcoal crayons, the ones he used in his talks explaining cave art. The sight of Véra with that wall full of holes behind her upsets me. The patches of bare brick remind me of the eerie ghost rocks I've seen in underground caves, phantom-like holes formed in thick subterranean rock by mineral dissolution. She's drawing mandalas on a poster for a 1999 production of *Three Sisters* at the theatre in Brive. She says she wants to use up the colour pencils so they don't go to waste. And how is using them like this not wasting them? I ask her. She gives me a wide-eyed look. I press the point, she shrugs, picks up another poster and carries on drawing. It's two o'clock in New York, I say. I have a video conference call. Véra says she doesn't mind. She never seems to mind, I think to myself as I turn on the computer in the bedroom. Nothing bothers her. It's not human, not my sister.

Feedback on episode four. Questions about the portrayal of the Second World War in light of the current situation in Europe. The people I'm speaking to have all blurred their background. Every time they move, their outlines wobble. One colleague reminds us that we're not making a documentary. But still, we can't sacrifice the complexity of reality to fiction. Someone says we should get back to the characters, we need to be more efficient, time is money. I don't make much of a contribution, I'm having problems with my microphone. I jump when I hear my name. One of the producers is suggesting that as a European, like Perec, I ought to have more of a personal connection to the project. I'm not sure I understand, I say. I peer closer to the camera, I don't think she can hear me. Their voices break up.

I'm bored, start browsing. My recent searches pop up. 'Before and after pregnancy', 'video Perec', 'weather Périgord', 'does he still love me'. I type in 'can you eat tripe' keeping one eye on the call. People's names are displayed as they speak, Laeticia's the most frequent. I've always liked the name Laeticia, it's soft and sharp at the same time. I hate my name, Agathe. It makes me think of an old lady with pointy glasses. Bitter. It sounds dry. It's softer in English, but I still don't like it. Agathe sounds like *agace*, irritate, annoy. I won't let Irvin say it.

There was a Laeticia in the skating group above mine. We'd run into each other in the changing rooms. She wasn't particularly talkative, but the other girls all fought for her attention. I'd heard about the parties she had at her parents' château, where there were always dozens of guests. I was amazed by the number of people she had in her circle. She had a boyfriend too. That left us all speechless. It didn't bother me that she didn't invite me. I had Véra for company, that was all I needed. But it was hard work communicating with my sister, I had to make most of the effort. I read something about sign language once and thought it might help, at least Véra would have a proper language. I mentioned it to my father and he took us to a talk about it. But Véra was adamantly against it. She refused to learn it, she wasn't deaf, she said.

The year I turned fourteen, I left our training session early one day to go to the toilet. When I came back I found Véra on the ice with my skates on. Laeticia's group was warming up. From where I was standing, Véra looked comical, like a drunken child. She was hanging onto Chloé, one of Laeticia's followers. I watched her fall, dragging Chloé down with her. Everyone froze. Véra let out a wail. Raw, animal-like, her cry amplified by the domed ceiling. Chloé got back up on her feet, rather exaggeratedly I thought, overplaying the effects of the fall.

'Idiot!' she spat out.

I said that Véra was sorry. Chloé said she wanted to hear Véra say it herself.

'She doesn't speak,' I replied.

'She can shout, can't she? So she must be able to speak.'

Chloé was standing with me at the edge of the ice rink. Véra was crawling towards us. I held out my hand to her. Laeticia skated over to Véra to help her reach me.

'Why doesn't she speak?' Chloé asked.

'She'd rather keep quiet than say the kind of things you do,' I quipped unthinkingly, thrown off balance by the mixture of jealousy and gratitude I felt towards Laeticia.

Chloé looked me up and down and smiled.

'You mean she's dumb?'

'She understands everything you say.'

Véra was smiling too, wringing her hands, her hair straggling around her face like wilted flowers.

'You understand what I'm saying?' Chloé barked at her.

I hated that smile of Véra's. I wished she'd start shouting again. Chloé shot me a look of triumph.

I slapped her.

'Leave it,' Laeticia said to Chloé. 'She can't help it.'

I led Véra towards the exit. I'd started feeling angry at Laeticia now too. She could have silenced Chloé earlier. She'd let me humiliate myself.

'You should've asked me first,' I said to Véra once we were on the bus.

The road was getting bumpy. I kept my eyes fixed straight ahead to stop myself feeling sick as the bus rattled along.

That evening, I pushed the living-room furniture aside, put on a recording of Dvořák and took hold of Véra, anchoring her back against my body. I explained to her that the trick to staying upright on ice skates is to imagine a block of ice in your abdomen. I showed her how to do it:

'Extend your arm. Legs straight.'

She had no sense of rhythm. I taped her ankles to mine and fell almost immediately, landing with my full weight on top of her. She was gasping for breath. I untangled her hair and realised she was laughing. I joined in. We carried on, collapsing again every time we looked at each other. I laughed so hard my ribs started to ache. I didn't notice Véra tying our wrists tightly together. My fingers were tingling.

'Stop it!' I cried.

She went on laughing. With a sudden jerk, I ripped open the ties, pulling out the hairs on my wrist.

I go out on the terrace with a cup of herbal tea, my brain fuzzy from the video call. A bat flits by, the security light comes on, triggered by a passing badger. He makes for the van and burrows underneath it.

My thoughts turn to Octave. The kitten. Did he know about it? We never mentioned it. The day we found the kitten I'd gone over to see him with a book he wanted to borrow from my father. He was a frequent visitor to our house, he came over to talk to my father, usually about things to do with archaeology. I'd hang around and listen and sometimes I joined in. I'd await his visits with a mixture of eagerness and embarrassment. Véra's presence weighed on me when I was with him. I hated the way my father talked about me, saying what a good big sister I was and boasting about my achievements at school and on the ice. It meant nothing, Octave was an adult and to him I was nothing but a fourteen-year-old kid.

I'd gone over to the château that day. It was the first time I'd ever really been alone with him. Mewling sounds came from the stables. There was a kitten lying in one of the stalls, it couldn't have been more than a month old. When it saw us it started wailing even louder and tried to bury itself under the straw. Octave knelt down, placed his hand on the kitten's back and kept it there until eventually the mewling began to quieten. Then he picked up the kitten and held it in the palm of his hand for me to stroke. I ran my fingertips over the trembling kitten, all I could feel were fur and vertebrae. We took it into the kitchen and tried to feed it. Octave dipped his finger in some milk and offered it to the kitten but it didn't even open its mouth. I thought Octave was pushing too hard but eventually, after several attempts, the kitten put out its long pink tongue, licked Octave's finger and threw itself at the saucer of milk. There was no question of Octave taking the little creature with him to Limoges where he was studying, and his family wasn't interested. He took hold of my arms and wrapped them around the kitten. He was certain I would take good care of it.

The little cat spent all its time hiding under the furniture, snarling whenever we came close. We couldn't get it to swallow the worming pills, it was still scrawny and flea-ridden and I was convinced we'd failed. On rare occasions it would come and curl up on my lap, pawing at me, drooling and purring loudly. Véra and I would both freeze, terrified of interrupting this miraculous event. I hoped the kitten would be equally affectionate towards her. One evening, as it was purring and pawing at me, Véra held out her hand close to it. We still hadn't given it a name, we wanted to get to know it first. The little cat stopped purring. Véra must have grabbed it as it was trying to get away, the cat clawed at her, fighting for all it was worth. Véra kept tightening her grip, I could see how distressed they both were, it upset me too and I shouted at her to let it go, for heaven's sake. The cat fell, landing on its belly. For a moment it didn't move. It spent the next two days in hiding under the wardrobe. I watched Véra surreptitiously all evening. I had a feeling she hadn't simply let go of the cat. She'd given it a push. Directed its fall. She'd thrown it to the ground.

Véra is lying on the sofa, my laptop open in front of her. I touch her shoulder, tell her I'm going up to bed. She barely stirs. Very carefully, I take the computer from her hands and cover her with my coat.

I look at my emails, hoping for a message from Irvin. The browser is open at the last page Véra was looking at. A video about sophrology. I can't resist the temptation to glance through her search history. Nothing but information about plants I've never heard of: Fremontodendron, Mahonia, Mexican orange. I scroll down to my own searches, blood rushing to my cheeks as I realise I hadn't deleted any of it. She must have seen it.

I muse about the course Véra's taking. Flower stabilisation. I google it. The stem of a flower is dipped in a liquid containing glycerine, colouring agents and nutrients. The glycerine enables the plant to retain water and absorb nutrients during the process of stabilisation. It takes several days. There are various techniques depending on the variety of flower and the desired result. Mosses still give the most reliable results.

10 NOVEMBER

Earlier this morning I thought I heard Véra in the shower. I realised after a while that it was the wind I was hearing. It blows up against the front of our house, rolling over like a swimmer turning in the pool. Véra is working on clearing the bathroom. I'm busy taking down posters, using a knife to scrape off the adhesive. The wall seems unnaturally soft, its surface crumbling to dust. I scrape until I hit something that seems solid. Sunflowers fall to the ground, exposing the network of cables threaded between the bricks, a nervous system laid bare.

We keep the door open, a warm breeze blows through

the living room. The birdcage sways, my hair lifts, the house seems to be breathing a sigh of relief. I'm tired. I was dreaming about the planet of mirrors. I'd shattered them all by banging into them. I was walking on broken glass, my feet bloodied. Shards of glass were digging into my flesh, working their way up through my veins and around my body, I looked unrecognisable.

We snack on prunes steeped in spices, with walnuts and cheese. I eat hungrily. Véra teases me, I've finished all Octave's jam. We'll have to do some shopping.

I sit at the table to do some work, Véra on the floor in the field of discarded posters. She's used up more than half of the charcoal pencils. I read over what I've written, whispering the words to myself to hear the rhythm: 'Afraid? Of what? That people might encroach on my territory? What territory? Somewhere to call home? A place to share, to defend and maybe even destroy? The only home I have is my language. My refuge. Words that hurtle into walls and fall to pieces.'

What's that you're working on? Véra asks, using her charcoal pencil to write the question.

Still deep in concentration, I mutter:

'A voiceover ... in the present ... visuals in flashback ...'

Is it me? Véra asks.

I sit up straight:

'Who?'

The girl, the backward one.

'What on earth are you talking about?'

In your film!

The film that's just won an award in Italy. So, she has seen it, I think to myself. I'm not sure if I should feel honoured or just embarrassed. I point out that the character she's referring to isn't backward, she's just afraid of her own feelings. She feels things intensely. The problem is that the film scripts are written by the whole group, I lose track sometimes. I show her my screen. Véra asks why I write only dialogue. It's only temporary, I explain, we share out our roles depending on the project. And despite what I just said, it's usually better working in a group.

Can I help?

I hate myself for laughing. The last thing I want is to be condescending. Véra examines the posters all around her. *The Bald Soprano*; an adaptation of Spiegelman's *Maus*. She lies down under the table and closes her eyes, hands resting on her chest.

'What are you doing?'

She puts a finger to her lips. I repeat my question. Visibly annoyed, she scribbles:

Shhhh!!! Bat concert.

Ten minutes later, still lying under the table, she starts tracing rapid circles around her navel with one finger. I can't help laughing but I'm worried about her getting cold. She pretends to chew, traces the line of her oesophagus and starts the circling motion again.

'Stop it! You'll make yourself ill!'

She turns over on her stomach, wiggling her legs as she writes:

Digestion accelerator.

She asks me to leave her alone.

I go back upstairs to the bedroom. I lie on the floor and try doing the same thing. Through the window I can see the bamboo bending in the wind, the hazelnut tree shivering. The chestnut tree towers over them, the master of ceremonies. You've been sleeping next to that tree for the last four nights, I think to myself. You're midway through your stay. You're closer to that tree than you are to your sister.

Later, in the supermarket, Véra piles food into the trolley. We're at the shopping centre just off the main road. I ask her to put some of it back. She claims we need it, sends me off to find things I like. I pick up some brioche buns, bananas, rice pudding. I'm a bit stiff from lying on the floor earlier. I can still feel the floorboards against the back of my head, my shoulder blades, buttocks and heels.

At the checkout, Véra places some little crumpled balls that look like dried persimmons on the conveyor. She's excited about them. They're candied mandarins. I watch couscous going past, chickpeas, coriander. I insist on paying again, even though I realise it makes me look as if I'm trying to make up for something.

Véra drives. Her car seems old to me with its roll-down windows. Not that I know much about these things. Disinfectant wipes, chewing gum, parking tickets in the glove pockets. The clock on the dashboard is slow, twelve minutes behind the time on our phones. I start trying to put it right but Véra stops me, she's used to it. She seems jumpy, something has shifted since this morning. The look in her eyes, more furtive. Twice, I've caught her glancing at my stomach.

'Do you mind if I put the radio on?'

Local news. The drought, fruit and vegetable growers' concerns. A door from a late Gothic château, missing since it was mysteriously stolen one night in 1928, has been found in the US. The government is calling for public funding to repatriate it.

Véra asks me for the scarf that's on the back seat. Brochures spill out onto the floor. An exhibition of orchids in Brantôme, wine cellars. Some have slipped under the seat. I can't reach them with my seatbelt on. Gusts of wind blow leaves onto the carriageway, Véra concentrates on the road ahead. Eventually, after much hesitation, I venture:

'Would you like it if I came to visit you?'

Her silence makes me wonder if I spoke at all. Finally, without taking her eyes off the road, she signals no and turns up the radio.

I don't say anything else after that.

I grab the door for support as we approach the steep slope going up to the house; I don't know why I do that, Véra is a good driver. We park under the hazelnut tree, the radio is still on, a debate about hunting. Véra mimes bringing the boxes outside to clear a space in the living room. I have doubts about the weather. She thinks it'll be fine. I tell her I'll help her but I need to do some work first. She waves her hands to say no, she'll manage on her own, she just wanted to make sure I agree.

'No, I'll help you. I can't do it now, but I will, later. You wanted me to come, and I'm here to help, there are two of us now, we've only got three more days.'

She reaches for her phone:

That's OK, I'll do it. I only asked you to be polite.

'For fuck's sake, Véra, I'm your sister!'

I can feel myself trembling. Véra shakes her head: no. She types something on her phone, deletes it and starts again several times, breathing heavily. I get out of the car and go upstairs to the bedroom, almost in tears.

The stairs creak. It's all such a muddle. Irvin. My being here. What did I expect? It's all because of Véra, I think to myself. Everything. My phone vibrates.

Why are you being so horrible?

I write straight back.

Horrible?!

You act like I don't exist. You don't tell me anything.

I get up to open the door. Véra is sitting at the top of the stairs, knees drawn up to her chin. I wonder what it is she wants me to tell her. Earlier, in the car, I was trying to talk to her. On the bed, my phone vibrates again. I look at Véra, wait for her to hold up her screen to me as she usually does. She points to the bed. I give in and pick up the phone.

`You feel obligated.`

'That's not true!'

I ask her quietly why she doesn't want me to come to her place.

`You're my sister. You're not my friend.`

Panic rises in my gut. I go and sit down next to her.

`I've got nothing to be ashamed of.`

'Why do you say that?'

`You were ashamed of me before. Now you feel sorry for me.`

Silence.

She's wrong, I murmur. She clamps her hands over her ears. Her phone falls down the stairs. The case comes off and bounces all the way to the kitchen. Now Véra is shaking too. At this moment, I want nothing more than for her to take me in her arms, but she pushes me away, so I stand up and spit out:

'You know nothing about my life either.'

11 NOVEMBER

Véra is downstairs in the living room, I'm up in the bedroom trying to do some work. The wind howls. When I hear Véra going into the bathroom I go down to make myself a coffee. I take it back up with a slice of toast and jam. If our paths cross, she ignores me.

Last night, we took the boxes outside together. The living room is empty now except for the table and chairs, armoire and sofa.

It's almost dark outside, I can see my reflection in the window, superimposed on the chestnut tree. The lampshade on the ceiling light is like an eyelid, the fabric fringe its eyelashes. Véra comes up looking for me. She's going for a walk, would I like to go with her? I'm really sorry, I say, gesturing towards my laptop. Almost immediately I regret saying no and set off to try and catch her.

There's no sign of her at the pond.

I strike out along a track I don't recognise, pushing aside the undergrowth as I go. The path follows a dried-up river bed. A sandy stretch leads to a barn with crumbling lime-washed walls. The sand makes me think of horses in a paddock. Darkness gathers, engulfing the forest, the trees grow denser, the ferns dusty and grey. In the half-light I glimpse something that looks to me like bones, a web of interlaced skeletons. If I knew the names of all these plants would they seem less menacing? Nature for me was always something my father told us tales about. I've never felt the need to label any of it with scientific terms. Whereas in the human world, I'm obsessed with precision. I pore over dictionaries, weigh up synonyms, compare the most subtle of nuances and meanings.

A man in an orange jacket walks by, his face weather-beaten. He plunges into the bushes. A few seconds later I hear a gunshot. Less than ten metres away. The man reappears. He speaks into a headset, says something that sounds like: 'Got it.' He's followed by a woman with white hair and leathery skin, carrying a gun pointed downwards. They're both wearing knee-high boots. I'm shaken, waiting for them to explain why this shot was fired so close to me when I was clearly visible. They walk on, paying no attention to me.

I hear the sound of a car and walk towards it, propelled by an urgent need to escape the woods. Out on the road the wind has turned colder, as if it's had a change of heart. Rain begins to fall. Cars whoosh past in a roar of rushing water, honking at me – I'm not wearing reflective clothing. I come to a hamlet that looks familiar. New houses, stone-coloured, a single lamppost. Dogs hurl themselves against fencing as I walk by, one barks and others follow suit. Windows open, someone shouts:

'Shut up!'

I walk up to one of the barking dogs. Its tail whips through the air, the dog is drooling, glistening with sweat and rain. I can feel its breath through the wire fencing. I murmur that I'm not going to hurt it. The dog flings itself at me, sinks its teeth into the metal, wild-eyed. I take a deep breath:

'I'm not going to hurt you . . .'

A woman wearing a tracksuit appears on a balcony:
'Hey, cut it out! OK?'

I slip away, my hood pulled up. The dogs go on barking, the sound gradually fading. I can hear shots now from another direction, a different hill. I head for the Pigeon Froid and think of Octave, comforted by the image of his large frame. Past the hamlet, a roadside sign: LEATHER. Two hangar-like structures, floodlit. Two lorries disgorging their load of pelts. Through the open doors I can see a mass of fabrics. I'm drawn in by the array of patterns and textures beyond anything I've ever imagined. At the other end of an aisle, an older man wearing snakeskin ankle boots arranges a display of lacquerware. Without turning round, he asks me what I'm looking for. I'd like to see the leather, I say. He looks me up and down, sizing me up: long coat, trainers, wet hair.

'Where did you spring from?'

His brusque familiarity puts me at ease.

'The US,' I say, 'but I was born here. Well, not here exactly, in Sarlat.'

'Sarlat! Well, that's completely different. That's Périgord Noir and this is Périgord Vert. Not the same at all.'

I smile, he's right. He goes back to arranging his display.

'So,' he says, 'what can I do for you today?'

'I write stories,' I say. 'What do you do here?'

His face lights up.

'You'll have to write something about our business then,' he says.

He explains that he's the son, he can show me around. Their business is leather. We go up to the first floor. Thousands of skins: cowhides, sheepskins, fish skins, reptile skins, stretched over frames supported by four legs. A museum of skins. The man starts talking as if his life depended on it. These buildings were part of a farm his parents turned into a salvage yard. During the war his mother collected rabbit pelts. They began by salvaging discarded animal skins from all over France and now, he declares proudly, they're the country's biggest supplier of skins to artisans and creators. He keeps up his running commentary as we follow a walkway leading to another building.

'Chanel, Vuitton, they don't know what they're losing with their offcuts,' he says. He shows me a particularly fine skin, dotted with tiny black marks, asks me to feel it:

'Stillborn. Veal,' he says and adds conspiratorially: 'That's when . . .'

'I know,' I say, cutting him off. 'You're right, though. It really is soft.'

He's thrilled: craftsmen can't get enough of it, he says. Finally, in his office, he shows me his most prized product, the desk mat made of salmon skin.

'Touch it,' he says. 'Can you feel the scales? How soft they are?'

Then he tells me times are hard, people don't want real leather anymore.

'You will write about it, won't you? Even though it's not exactly headline news.'

And with that, he escorts me to the door and leaves me outside under the lights that line the road.

The trees form a protective tunnel overhead as I walk. I arrive at the château almost completely dry. A deer has sought shelter near the front gate. It's raining so hard he doesn't hear me coming. He's standing, nibbling at a bush, only three or four metres away from me. He's huge, definitely a male. I've never been this close to a deer before. A hunting horn sounds in the distance. The deer looks up, goes back to nibbling the bush. We stay there, neither of us moving. I try coming a little closer. Only two metres, I could almost reach out and touch him. Then he sees me and bounds off.

There's no answer from Octave when I press the buzzer but the gate isn't locked. I step into the courtyard and glance towards the open stable door. I can see the donkey and llama huddled at the back of the stall. No car. It's raining too hard to walk all the way over to the house. I decide to seek refuge in the pigeonnier. The courtyard is awash with water, the pigeonnier surrounded by fast-flowing rivulets. The tarpaulin slaps against the scaffolding revealing occasional glimpses of the doorway, a black rectangular void. I venture inside and take in my surroundings. A platform of about two square metres overhangs a pit that used to collect droppings from the pigeons that nested in the hundreds of small recesses cut into the walls all the way up to the roof. Their rounded shapes make me think of a wine cellar. The ground is spotless. I'm a little disappointed. There's nothing here to conjure up the fire except perhaps the small holes high up under the roof. Those holes will be filled with the stones from our house. I climb up a rickety ladder, sit on one of the beams and look out at the courtyard. The rain is still lashing down. The streams of water have formed a moat around the tower. A car pulls up. I wave my phone in the air, making wide sweeping gestures. Octave flashes his headlights in response. He pulls his hood up and runs over to join me.

'It's really coming down, isn't it?' I shout.

I can hear him shaking off the rain. The ladder vibrates, firm footsteps. Octave sits down beside me, backpack on his knees.

'You're crazy coming up here. Were you planning to fly away, or what?'

'Do I look that unhinged?'

He looks down at my hand pressed to my chest. My heart is going a mile a minute. I tell him about the gun, the shot that narrowly missed me.

'Oh, yeah. It's Armistice Day.'

'What's that got to do with hunting?'

'People hunt on all public holidays. And Wednesdays, when the children are off school.'

I move a little to one side, water is running off our raincoats and forming a small puddle.

'How many birds were here back in the day?'

Octave produces a torch from his bag and shines it towards the middle of the tower. There were 1,417 pigeonholes when it was built, he says, each one with a nest. Not so many now, the wall is too damaged. I do some quick calculations:

'Almost three thousand pigeons in such a small space...'

Octave directs his beam towards my chest and declares that I really should be wearing a fluorescent jacket.

'But it's our forest,' I say, on the defensive. 'We live here!'

'I know...'

'What about you? What were you doing out there?'

'I was on the lookout for a turkey.'

I burst out laughing.

'Seriously,' he says. 'A friend's turkey ran away during the festival in Varaignes. In all the excitement.' He pauses for a moment. 'He was very attached to it,' he adds.

'Ah, it was today, then. Are they still doing the imitation-turkey-gobbling competition?'

'You know about that?'

'I grew up around here too,' I say indignantly. 'The Grand International Festival of Périgord Turkeys!' I proclaim loudly.

He doesn't know it, but for the two years before I left for the US, Octave's presence there was the only reason I went to the fair. But for him, I would never have gone. We did occasionally run into each other but I was always flanked by my sister and Octave was usually off to one side, in the pear orchard, with his friends.

'Did you find the turkey?'

'No, but I did see you.'

'You did? Just now, in the woods?' I reply innocently.

He smiles, takes what looks like another torch out of his bag and asks me if I've ever looked through a thermal imaging camera. He adjusts the settings and hands it to me.

A lunar landscape comes into view. Sources of heat are lit up, the stable, château, forest, their outlines wavering, as if the whole scene might explode at any moment. I become aware of how high up we are here in the pigeonnier, the castle walls built into the rock. The pond in the background is black, like the sky, it must be freezing cold. Something is glowing in the darkness. I adjust the focus. The statue. Pure white. I'm amazed that it gives out so much heat.

'The stone absorbs heat,' Octave says.

'Where did it come from, the statue?'

He says it was always there, before his family. His grandmother had it restored in the 1960s. 'There were other figures too, statues of cherubs, men.'

'What happened to them?'

'I don't know. When the old owners were here there were elm trees where the water is now.'

'Elm trees?'

'It's an artificial lake.'

I point the camera back towards the courtyard. The donkey and llama have moved closer to the doorway. I focus in on them, unnerved by how clearly they stand out. They look like targets in a video game, a shooting game. I turn the camera towards Octave and look away immediately, dazzled by the brilliance of the image.

'You see that? How bright people are?' he says. 'You look like you're on fire.'

I put the camera down and look around for Octave and realise I can't see. Everything has gone black. I reach out, groping. He takes my arm:

'Don't worry, that always happens.'

I force myself to believe him. My vision is already coming back in the eye that wasn't looking through the viewfinder, but everything is darkened, like wearing sunglasses at night. I'm still blind in the other eye.

'The retina needs time to adjust,' Octave says.

I sense his warmth. His gentleness calms me. I breathe in his smell, mingled with the smell of rainwater, both intensified by his waterproofs. I feel an urge to press myself to him, have him hold me in his arms. I ask him about his work. His voice takes on a less serious tone. He talks about orchids, the disappearing limestone grasslands, the dwindling peatlands. He says he's hungry and asks me if I feel like having something to eat. Straight away I think of Véra and decide I'll message her from the château. Octave helps me down the ladder. The donkey brays.

'Why do you have a llama?'

'It belonged to a neighbour. When he died, I decided to keep it.'

The kitchen seems smaller and more functional than the way it used to be. It could be anywhere, like the kitchen in the apartment I share with Irvin in New York. Octave feeds another log into the stove, offers me some olives, starts chopping something that smells like fennel. He says he's been doing a bit of research. My remarks the other day had prompted him to think about the name of the château, or the châtelet as he calls it.

'Why do you call it a châtelet? It sounds funny.'

'Because you don't hear it very often? It's just an old word for a small castle, but the Pigeon Froid isn't really big enough even to be called a châtelet. Originally, there was just the tower. The farm buildings were added on several hundred years later. It was known as Puy Geoffrey – puy is an old Occitan word for hill. Geoffrey must have been the name of the guy who lived there. When the government decided to survey the countryside, they sent officials from Paris who heard it as "Pigeon Froid". That's how they recorded it on their maps and it became the official name. There are dozens of stories like that.'

I ask him why he wants to use the stones from my house. He says they're from the same period as the pigeonnier, our house is a goldmine. I laugh and tell him he shouldn't delude himself. He doesn't agree. You never know, he says. He found two skeletons when he was repairing the tower, in a sarcophagus. Children. They were lying head to toe, he'd never seen skeletons laid out like that before.

'What did you do with them?'

'I gave them to the museum in Périgueux but then the police started investigating all the unsolved cases from the last thirty years and I came under suspicion. They called me in for questioning. It went on for three months. The whole thing was ridiculous, and ultra-stressful. Those skeletons are a thousand years old.'

'What, you mean they didn't believe you?' I say, shocked.

He laughs.

'They had to in the end. The forensic experts confirmed that the skeletons were much too old for the cases the police were investigating.'

He explains that he doesn't want to apply to any official body to restore the property. He'd have to register it as a national monument and that would mean all sorts of restrictions and regulations; everything would have to conform to the standards of a particular period. He prefers to do it unofficially, it's simpler that way. It was my father who encouraged him to do the renovations, he says.

'I have a lot to thank him for,' he adds. 'He had a thing about the pigeonnier.'

I can't help but smile.

'That story about the fire that was never explained,' he goes on. 'He kept coming back to it.'

'Yes, he did.'

'With you and your sister too?'

I don't say anything. I can hear my father's laugh. Rich. Deep. Him talking about the pigeonnier. The bricked-up doorway. My eyes have finally adjusted and I watch Octave peeling blood oranges. Spread out on the table all around him are pieces of wood, samples, each with a label.

'What are you laughing at?' he asks me.

'That name. Alnus glutinosa.'

'Alder trees. There are lots of them near your place.'

He uses the plural form for 'your'. He means mine and Véra's. It bothers me when he does that. I lean down to examine another piece of wood, decorated with an elegant engraving in the shape of a spider.

'This one. What's this?'

'Elm. A relic. They were almost completely wiped out in the 1970s by graphiosis. Dutch elm disease.'

'What's that?'

'A fungal infection. You can tell from the patterns in the wood – the fungus does that.'

'Graphiosis,' I murmur to myself. 'Sounds like a disease of writing.'

Octave looks up again briefly. He asks me about my films, what drives me. Coming from him, the question doesn't annoy me the way it usually does. But my stomach still seizes up. I answer in vague terms, I say there's a lot to manage at the moment. He wants to know if that's because of the house, whether leaving it is too much of a strain.

'No, it doesn't bother me. But Véra on the other hand . . .'

I shouldn't hesitate to ask him for help, he says. My sister and I are pretty tough, I respond. I know, he says.

He pours us both some wine. I look around, searching for clues about his life, his relationship. Apricot kernels on the worktop, set out to dry. Bottles of homemade fruit juice. Several wooden pepper grinders. Jars of jam lined up on the floor against the walls.

'Apricot,' says Octave. 'And rosehip.'

My mouth waters at the thought of their sharp taste. I realise I'm very hungry. I tell Octave how grateful I am for everything he does for us in my absence. For my father and Véra. He's hardly done anything, he says. Véra manages just fine. He's even felt sometimes that she keeps him at arm's length. She's always been polite but she doesn't smile very much.

Véra's smile.

I feel a mounting sense of sadness. Octave is talking about my father's gradual decline, the shock of the sudden end. I'm having difficulty listening to him. I try and jump back in, asking questions without taking in what he says in response.

'. . . you were his favourite.'

'What?'

Octave says it couldn't have been easy for Véra, growing up with a sister as brilliant as me. What does he know about it? I think to myself. It occurs to me that I've never heard a man paying me a compliment in French. He refuses my offer of help setting the table, puts the fennel in the oven. My cheeks are flushed from the wine. I lean back against the counter. He's rolled up his sleeves, I can see his shirt under the jumper. The plates seem heavy but he doesn't bang them down on the table, he places them with hardly a sound.

'Do you know the history of the pigeonnier?' I ask him.

'That's just it, no one has ever really . . .'

I take a deep breath and start reciting, doing my best to inject a note of mystery into my voice:

'Pigeonniers were constructed to enable the wealthiest members of society to witness the breeding habits of pigeons.'

Octave sits down at the table, turns sideways to face me and rests one arm on the table. I continue, doing my best to enunciate clearly, staring at the window to help myself concentrate:

'It was a thing of beauty to behold. Pigeons were a rare and highly prized species. They carried messages, their meat could be eaten and even their droppings were collected to fertilise the soil. So soft and gleaming were their feathers, the trees themselves grew branches for them to nest in. A pigeon's life was brief and when one died another would die of grief soon afterwards. But the will to live is strong and the species found a way to survive. When two pigeons came together in love, their amorous caresses were so ardent the birds would catch fire. Such was the heat of their passion, they felt no pain. Locked in loving embrace, the birds were consumed by the flames. When they died, all that was left was an intricately woven pile of bones. But among those bones was a fertile cinder from which an egg would emerge. Ash penetrated the shell and nourished the baby bird, which took on the colour of those ashes. The centuries passed and now when we gaze at the shimmering blue-grey hues of our pigeons' feathers, we see the reflected glimmer of those flames.'

A crease has formed in Octave's forehead. I sit down at the table with him. He pours us some more wine. The room is warm. Condensation trickles down the window. I confess that this story was one of my father's.

'I didn't know he was a storyteller.'

'You didn't? He was always telling stories.'

Octave is surprised. He'd always considered my father to be a model of scientific rigour. I'm surprised too, that Octave never saw that other side of my father.

His phone rings. He should answer it, I say. He apologises, says it's probably his girlfriend. I leave the room. I'm not sure how I feel about being here. I send Véra a message to say I'll be back late. There's a message from Irvin. I hesitate. I'll read it later. Out in the hallway it's much colder, there's no heat here. I rub my arms, stare at the pictures on the wall. Drawings, signed and dated, Italian names, recent dates. There used to be old portraits here. I wait for a while before I go back in, I want to be sure I don't interrupt Octave. When I do go back, he's already served up the fennel and lentils.

'Everything OK?'

We laugh, we've both spoken at the same time. He gestures to me to eat, waits for me to start. I ask him about his girlfriend. She's a colleague of his at the university, he says. She lives in Bordeaux, they don't see each other very often.

'And everything is OK?' I ask again.

He asks me to please eat, it'll get cold. The pepper makes me cough. The food is delicious.

'If you had to choose,' he says, 'would you rather be desired for your whole life, without being loved? Or would you prefer to be loved, like a friend?'

I'm not sure I understand.

'That's what she asked me just before she left on holiday. . .'

'And what about your little girl? How does that work?'

He says he has to tread carefully. I nod slowly in agreement.

'The other day she told me I'd never be her dad.'

'She's not your daughter?'

He looks wary. I mumble something, embarrassed. It's all right, he says, he didn't make himself clear. Basically, he's happy with the situation. He didn't necessarily want to have a child. Swann was three when he met her mother. She's nearly six now. It's getting easier now that they can actually have a conversation, and he thinks she likes talking to him. He laughs:

'Well, I thought she did. And what about you?'

'Me?'

He gives me a kindly look.

'Véra tells me you've met someone nice.'

What right does she have to talk about me? I think to myself. But I nod in agreement.

'When are you leaving?'

'On the fourteenth.'

'And everything is fine?'

I tease him about the way we keep asking each other the same questions. Like mirror images. Now it's his turn to look flustered. I touch his arm lightly, as if to reassure him, tell him it's all fine. He stares at me. He's searching for confirmation that I'm telling the truth.

I think about Irvin and our upcoming anniversary. In three days' time it will be eight years since we met.

I start talking about my life in America, about the film industry, how hard it is for people to relate. We move the conversation to more light-hearted topics, but we're both still in serious mode. My stomach feels bloated, it's been like that every evening lately, my trousers too tight. I rearrange my jumper, trying to hide my stomach.

After dessert I make an early exit. I thank him and say I have to leave because of Véra. She hasn't answered my message. But the truth is that I've had enough, I don't want to be here anymore, with Octave, I've had enough of this house and all these old stories. I'm back to being fifteen years old again, asking him to come and pick me up outside the cathedral. I'm wearing my smartest skating skirt, lacy tights, amber necklace. My lips are chapped. Octave sitting on my left, driving in silence, me asking him to please not say anything to my father, the look he gives, the same look he gave me just now when he asked me how I am. I still don't know what he thinks of me. But it doesn't really matter now, my life is elsewhere, on another continent.

The rain has eased up. I can walk home on my own, I say firmly. Octave lends me the thermal camera, gives me a jar of jam, which I ask him to open. He screws the lids on too tight for me. He comes with me for part of the way. We walk slowly. After the gate I stop and look up at his face in the half-light. A line from the filmscript runs through my mind. I plant a kiss on his cheek, near his ear:

'Some people say that when you truly love someone, you're less likely to say what you really think.'

The Christmas holidays had begun. Laeticia was having a party and I was invited; I found the invitation slipped into my skate. The location was a secret, my instructions were to wait in the cathedral square where someone would come and pick me up. It was soon after the incident with Véra, I'd just turned fifteen and I knew I was leaving for the US in six months. I felt excited all week, but I was nervous too, I'd never been out on my own before. I told Véra I had late practice. I gave her instructions for the lasagne and promised I'd be home by ten. I'd definitely be back before my father. I said nothing to him about it – he was working late doing sound and light shows in the run-up to Christmas.

I got changed in a corner of the cathedral. Pearl-embroidered jumper, tulle skirt, an old amber necklace of my mother's. I'd let my hair down, it smelt of shampoo. I went outside to wait in the square. I was the first to arrive but it was still early. I wandered around the Christmas market set up in the car park. I'd bought a lipstick and kept checking to see what it looked like. I eyed my reflection in mirrors on jewellery stalls, in stained glass windows, pieces of handblown glass, any reflective surface I could find. The crowd was thinning out. I went back to the steps in front of the cathedral. At quarter past six I checked the invitation to make sure I was in the right place. All around me the stall holders were starting to pack up. The lights would go on flickering all night. I was afraid to go inside the cathedral to warm up in case I missed the meet-up. I started thinking there must be a mistake on my invitation. Maybe the party was starting an hour later, the other girls were all good friends, they'd spread the news by word of mouth. I didn't have their phone numbers.

By now, the streets were deserted. The night was freezing. At seven o'clock, a bus came sputtering into the square, two people got off and hobbled towards the centre of town. The wind was icy, my limbs felt stiff from the cold, my fingers so numb I couldn't open my bag. Eventually I went inside the cathedral. The nativity scene that year was more traditional than usual. Natural clay figurines, their features roughly hewn. I stole one of the shepherds to take back for Véra. As I detached the figurine from its base, a piece of cardboard tore off. I covered the hole with bits of straw.

When it eventually became clear that no one was coming, I sat down on one of the pews to think. A woman in a red coat came into the cathedral, my mother's age, heavily made up. Her footsteps rang out down the aisle. I could see the reflection of my lips in my phone's screen. The red had faded completely leaving only the flaking outline. I rubbed my lips. The skin felt soft, I imagined sinking my finger all the way in until it disappeared, or the skin stretching and becoming detached, like a balloon you could pierce with a needle. I heard cars passing, less and less frequently. The last bus had gone. My plan had been to find someone at the party to give me a lift home. The woman in the red coat left. I felt the vibrations as the great doors slammed shut, the sound echoing through the cathedral. It was Friday, Octave would be home. I scrolled through my contacts until I found his name.

He showed up thirty minutes later. He was in the middle of exam season, concentration etched into his features. I thanked him for coming. He was only too happy to help me out, he replied, his tone polite and formal. He drove me in silence, slipping stealthily from one gear to the next, while I sat beside him decked out in pearls and tulle, scarcely daring to look at him. In profile, his nose protruded sharply from his wool hat. He asked if I was all right. I nodded. A few moments later I muttered something about him not mentioning it to my father. Octave raised an eyebrow, eyes fixed on the road.

'Did you say something?'

'Don't say anything to my father,' I repeated, still barely audibly.

His Adam's apple moved, jaw clenched. He nodded. I turned to look out of the window. If only I could have at least pretended to be pleased with myself for going out in secret. I closed my eyes to avoid his gaze.

'Will you be all right?' he asked as we pulled up outside the house.

In my rush to get out of the car I slammed the door unintentionally. I turned back to open it again but the car was already moving off.

That night, Véra was waiting for me in the living room, red-cheeked, her jumper wet. She pointed to the bathroom. Water was splashed over the walls around the toilet, a towel was lying on the floor, sodden.

'What happened?' I asked. I had my suspicions.

Reluctantly, I peered into the toilet bowl. The kitten was floating in the water, its head and front paws sucked down into the U-bend. The toilet hadn't flushed completely. The thought occurred to me that maybe I should just give it another flush. I seized the kitten by the tail. There was a slight sucking sensation. I held it in my hand. So tiny, water-logged, its little jaw, eyes half-closed, bones as delicate as a dragonfly's. The little creature had been with us for a month. The previous evening, Véra and I had been joking that we'd probably always refer to it as 'the kitten'. I placed it on a fresh towel. Véra gulped, shaking. She was pinching her lips, knotting and unknotting her fingers. I drew closer to her, wanting to comfort us both, but her face suddenly changed. She took on a strangely neutral expression. I asked what had happened. And then, without waiting for her to reply, I said the kitten fell in, he was trying to drink and he slipped. All she had to do was nod in agreement. Véra was staring at me. I nodded, repeating what I'd just said, to convince myself it was true. Véra was beginning to scare me. I searched desperately for signs of pity in her. In the end, I murmured:

'What have you done?'

She opened her eyes wide. I took her head in my hands, squeezing as hard as I could, still nodding my head. I felt dizzy. With her cheeks pressed together she looked like she was smiling, the same blank smile I'd seen on her face in the refectory all those years earlier with Margaux, or with Chloé in the cloakroom of the skating rink. I shouted at her in frustration:

'He didn't even have a name!'

She made a gurgling sound. I let go of her.

We sat down on the couch, the kitten wrapped in the towel in my lap. I was exhausted. I heard the sound of our father's car. I shot Véra a defiant look.

'It was an accident,' I said as soon as he came in the door.

He placed two gift-wrapped packages by the hearth, took off his coat.

'It wasn't Véra's fault.'

'Girls . . .'

'He fell in by himself.'

My father leant on the table. He gave me a long look.

I lowered my gaze to the little wet bundle leaking onto my skirt. I realised I was still in my party clothes, wearing my mother's necklace. My father's disappointment. I told him everything. The invitation, the humiliation. How sorry I was. I'd been so excited. I thought it was all going to work out. Véra stood up. My father looked surprised, as if it had just sunk in. Véra had her back to me, breathing hard, she seemed to be gasping for breath. Wearily, he said that it wasn't enough to just imagine things. I didn't understand. He unwrapped the towel and brought us back to the real problem. Then, with barely a glance at the kitten, he went to put the kettle on. From the kitchen he announced that he relied on me. Véra and I couldn't have these arguments. He was sorry we were left alone so much but his work wasn't a game. It was no joke telling stories destined to be instantly forgotten by the people he told them to. He took it very seriously.

'Think of your sister.'

He went upstairs. Véra turned round to face me. She'd regained her composure. I followed my father up the first few stairs, the kitten in my arms. I shouted up to him that he knew nothing about my sister. Then, in a voice devoid of emotion, I said that she was ruining my life, I understood how our mother felt, I hated this house, I hated my sister, I wished she'd never been born, I'd had enough of doing everything I could to protect her, she was selfish, and worse than that she was stupid, yes, that's what she was, she was stupid, dumb, idiotic. Spitting out slugs, that's all she was good for. And as I spoke, I hated myself for even thinking such things.

In the plane on the way to the US I'd told myself that Véra had the power to make me have thoughts like that. She still does today. I stared at the rain-spattered window, watching as this country slipped from view.

When I get back to the house it's almost eleven o'clock. The van parked outside doesn't look sturdy enough to transport all the things piled into it. Véra has covered it all with a tarpaulin held down by rocks. I feel guilty about staying out so long. I go inside without bothering to turn on the lights. The smell of damp has been made worse by all the rain. Bread lies shrivelled on the table, a whitish mark beside it. At first I think the cheese must have run, but no, the cheese is safely stowed in the cage, and the stain doesn't smell. Wax from a melting candle, its wick still intact. I glance at my phone. Irvin's message. My heart starts pounding at the thought of reading it.

I sit down on the sofa and open the jar of jam. I'm not hungry at all. Octave has messaged me too. I don't know which one to read first. I decide to read Irvin's.

He asks how I am and signs himself 'Irvin'. I read it several times. The last time he signed a message with his name was before our first kiss.

Octave says he was glad to see me, we mustn't hesitate to call him, we know where to find him.

I feel frustrated towards both of them. I squeeze half a lemon to ward off feelings of nausea and eat a large spoonful of jam. The sugar makes my tongue tingle.

Véra's clothes are thrown on the floor in the bathroom. I undress in front of the mirror. My veins stand out against my pale skin. I turn the hot water up high, I'm so cold. You accuse me of not confiding in you, Véra, you say I'm distant. I don't know what to tell you about myself. You don't know about all the times I've spoken up for you to make your life more bearable. I've never acted out of pity, you're wrong about that, it was always to protect you. I wasn't strong enough to stay. That's why I'm incapable of talking to you. I'm going to leave again, and I need to know that you don't hate me. You have no idea how much I love you.

I'll always be there for you.

What a ridiculous thing to say.

What does it mean, to 'be there' for someone? I'm not there for you, I'm not there enough for Irvin, and I don't feel capable of being there for a child.

The shower drains slowly. I aim the water on full power at the drainage hole. The shower tray fills with water. The drain gurgles and spits out a ball of scum entwined with our hair. Long strands of hair that seem to have no beginning and no end come floating out. Neither Véra nor I have hair that long.

I lose track of time. My skin is flushed red. The steam thickens to form a dense cloud.

As I emerge from the shower, I notice some letters, traced with a finger, shining through the greasy surface of the mirror: sorry.

I turn over several times under the covers before settling down. I don't want to wake Véra. I can hear her breathing. I'm thirsty. I can't go back downstairs, the stairs would creak. Her breathing is calm but if I listen closely I can tell she's not asleep, she's breathing too rapidly. Now it's her wakefulness that stops me from getting up.

I'd like to know what it's doing to her, leaving this house. I thought I'd said goodbye to it fifteen years ago. I feel like going back downstairs, bringing all the things piled up outside back into the house, gathering up the dust from the charcoal pencils. I want the walls to go on crumbling behind the posters, the cage to rust away around the cheese, the house to smell to high heaven for ever. I want to know what my sister dreams of, if she too has visions of our father sleeping, his neck frail, the vein pulsing beneath his withered flesh. The breath flowing from his nostrils as if he is at peace. His body that seems to say: your father is no longer there, he is somewhere else, he lives in memory. I want to shout at him to wake up, I want to yell out his name, I want to say to my father: Stay. Stay here. But let me go.

Véra can't answer me in the dark, and I've had enough of the back and forth on our screens. I wait, for a long time. I don't know who falls asleep first.

I know Irvin is upset with me. My silence has hurt him.

The advice on forums online is to write it all down, to give a name to the person that might have been. To make someone exist. The idea seems false to me. But all the same, I spend hours searching for advice. I have to stop reading these things. I'd feel ridiculous writing to someone who has no meaning for me, someone I hadn't chosen as a companion. You are nothing to me. You've never been anything to me. I didn't choose you. But the more I search the more I think: who would you have been? Would I have been able to love you?

I didn't have to decide. My body chose for me.

That night, I didn't wake Irvin. I'd read that you mustn't fight grief, you must give it your full attention. I didn't wake Irvin because I didn't have the strength to reassure him. I waited for him to go to work and took the subway and then the bus to the hospital. The consultant told me there was still some foetal tissue left. A tablet would cause the remaining tissue to be expelled. Maternity ward. Women resting, newborn babies in their arms. I hear the clang of metal as my neighbour goes back and forth to the toilet. Nothing stirs in my womb. At seven o'clock in the evening they give me another dose. At eleven o'clock I still haven't lost a drop of blood. I go home. In the subway, I stare at the exit signs, focus on the words in English that have nothing to do with what has happened inside my body.

I started to haemorrhage the next morning. I was still bleeding after ten days. They had to operate. Only then did I tell Irvin.

We made love again when the bleeding stopped. For weeks, I seemed to have been invisible to Irvin. I took the initiative. He needed plenty of time to become hard in my mouth, to respond to my falsely joyous hands.

When I took him inside me, I tried to meet his gaze. His eyes were closed. I bore down harder, pressed my hips against his, leaned my face close to his. I was afraid to ask him to look at me. When I realised he wasn't moving with me, I closed my eyes too. I was glad his eyes were closed. That way he wouldn't see my tears.

Afterwards, I pulled on a T-shirt and went out onto the balcony, despite the cold. Smells of fat frying wafted from the air vents. I stayed out there for at least ten minutes, until I heard Irvin approaching. He wrapped his arms round me and led me back to bed.

I woke during the night to feel his body gently penetrating mine. I gave myself up to the slowness of the rhythm, intensifying every movement. Making it last longer. So long as we don't climax, we are together.

12 NOVEMBER

For once, I'm up before Véra. I wanted to set the table for breakfast. The smell of something rotting has become so strong in the kitchen I can hardly breathe. I'm beginning to wonder if the problem is with me, if it's all in my head. Véra wrinkles her nose when she comes down too and sets my mind at rest. She opens the empty armoire and sniffs the cheese, the mushroom basket, walks all around the fireplace. We're looking for something that's died. She gives up and shrugs: what's the point, we're leaving in two days.

We eat our toast, drink our coffee, exchange embarrassed looks. The rain drums against windows.

`How was it yesterday?` she writes.

I feel myself blushing. I start talking about my evening at Octave's, the improvised meal, exploring the pigeonnier. I get carried away, caught up in my account, tell her about the thermal camera. Véra listens, interested. She knows about thermal cameras, she uses them to locate hunters.

We go over what we still need to do. Load up the van, take out the furniture. Sort out our parents' bedroom. We clam up at the thought of doing this. I let Véra know that I absolutely have to do some work first, I haven't made much progress with the script.

The computer makes a whirring sound. I restart it. Outside, water spurts from the drainpipe onto the trunk of the chestnut tree. The moss grows thicker at this spot. Like the forehead of a stag, its antlers branching out in front of me.

I've barely started working when Véra bursts in excitedly. She brandishes an oozing mass in my face, a rotten mushroom, the culprit responsible for the foul stench, it's contaminated all the others, she's thrown them out. Well done, I say, pushing her arm away from my face. I'm afraid I might throw up all over her. She skips out of the room.

I open the window. A flurry of red ivy leaves scatters to the floor. I pick them up and put them on the chest of drawers. For a moment, they seem to throb, tiny hearts escaped from their cages to die.

I go back into the living room soon after noon. The floor is wet. Véra's mopped it. Now, she's perched on the stepladder in a cloud of dust, her head up the chimney, using her phone as a torch. She waves her free hand, gesturing to me to pass her the metal rod placed at her feet. Her fingers are shrivelled from the cold, her skin dry and scaly. I look down at my hands. I don't like them, I never have. I can't wear rings, my knuckles are too bony.

Véra comes down from the stepladder. I see with a shock that her hair is all grey. She heads for the bathroom, I follow her to look at myself in the mirror. I'm all grey too, we're both coated in ash. Véra takes off her jumper, gives it a shake in the shower cubicle. The lines in her smooth white skin stand out in sharp contrast, accentuated by the covering of ash. I can't help feeling that I've brought these lines into existence simply by staring at them. They'll never go away. We're old.

I point this out to Véra, who's gone back to peering up the chimney. She laughs, writes in ash on the wall: At long last!

Our parents' bedroom smells like a cellar where vegetables are stored. After my father's funeral, my mother came to collect some of her things. All that's left now is their great solid wooden bed with its two drawers. The bed is so heavy it's gouged dents into the floorboards. No one will ever be able to move it, not even Octave. Our initials are carved into each of the four legs: our parents', N and M, at the front, and ours at the back, A and V.

There's not much in the drawers: a few history and geography magazines, a packet of tissues, raspberry flavoured chews. I look up at Véra, surprise is etched into her face. She hands me a book. A memoir by an American explorer, dating back to the 1980s. A piece of card for a bookmark and an inscription in my father's writing: 'My darling princesses. Make sure you always go on loving one another. Don't waste your time on things that aren't worth it. I will always love you.' I glance through the page with the bookmark, searching for clues, something to indicate that my father wanted to talk to us. There's nothing, only a passage describing an ice field, the explorer following an animal's tracks.

We come across some old photographs wrapped in a linen cloth. A man and a woman, naked, limbs intertwined. Their faces are hidden but you can sense the intimacy of their rapport. In another photo, much more recent, a woman poses in front of the house in a white coat. It's dated ten months before my birth. I stare at the image. This woman, my mother. But not yet my mother. Véra and I hover above it, each holding one edge. Véra looks up at me, questioning. I shake my head, I haven't heard from her: has she? Slowly, she shakes her head. No, she hasn't either.

The mattress sags, it's too bulky to be rolled up. We don't have anything to strap it up with, it won't fit on the landing. Véra examines the French doors. My father installed them. There was always a window there but he made the opening bigger at my mother's request, not long before she left us. Did it have anything to do with her leaving? Véra gives me an enigmatic look and for a moment I think she might have read my mind.

The handle appears to be jammed. It's raining outside. Véra studies the doorframe, peering at something, pushes on it a little. I shout at her to stand back.

Too late, the nest has broken open. I watch the bees come spinning out, a graceful dance in slow motion, dreamlike. Véra joins the dance. She cries out, rousing me from my daze. I rush to find a blanket and wrap her in it. I lift her up and carry her out to the landing, struggling beneath her weight as I close the door behind us. I hear the bees buzzing inside the room. Véra clutches her head. I move her hands away. Her face is swollen and distorted.

I sit her on her bed, daub her with antiseptic cream and extract the stings with tweezers, I cover her eyes with a cloth soaked in warm water and apply dressings to the swellings. She presses my palm to her cheek. I'm undone by this gesture, I can't help feeling I tried to help her not so much to stop her from being stung, but because I couldn't bear to hear her cry out. I hate it. I prefer it when she stays silent.

Her eyes are closed. I stroke the back of her neck, observing her hairline, the sparse, thin hairs behind her ears, her forehead almost hairless. I'm moved by the randomness of this arrangement. I lean in closer and peer at the down on her upper lip, the blackheads on her nose. This eye, this mouth, this forehead – I have to keep telling myself: this is my sister.

I'm going to destroy the nest, I announce, and get up to go and look for some insect spray.

I feel sick just thinking about the smell. I hesitate. The bees won't survive the winter. We don't have to go back in there, we could leave the room as it is. But I open the door and go in anyway. Dead insects on the floor. A faint buzzing sound comes from the nest attached to the doorframe. I can see bees hovering around it. I give the spray a long squirt. Bees start flying out immediately. I run back out onto the landing slamming the door behind me. Instinctively I turn the lock.

We sit on Véra's bed listening. I imagine the carnage, bees attacking one another, their airways on fire.

'Does it hurt?'

Véra grabs an ivy leaf from the chest of drawers, examines the leaf lines, compares the patterns to the lines in our hands. She traces a series of letters into my palm with her fingertip. As soon as I understand I pull my hand away, protesting that the sore patch on my hand is not a wart.

On the other side of the wall, the noise has stopped, like the rain that's turned to mist. The chestnut tree has disappeared from view. The bedroom suddenly seems very dark to me.

'What shall we do with Maman and Papa's bed?'

The question hangs in the air. Véra glances at the computer, asks me if I'm making progress. I start talking about the script, the conflicting demands. A famous actor has finally accepted one of the main parts on condition that he appears in every episode. His character is supposed to die in the fourth episode. His significance only becomes clear in his absence, by implication. We have to rewrite everything, it's the only solution. Véra mimes waking up from the dead: are we going to bring him back to life? I shake my head. Out of the question. We can do it as memory, flashback.

On an impulse, I ask her if she wants to read what I've written, I can translate as she reads. Delighted, she takes my computer and places it on her lap. The look on her face makes me anxious, I start making excuses:

'They're saying my writing is too literary. It's ridiculous, I've always written for film. That's all I've ever done. The trick is to come up with something that's like real life even though it's not real . . .'

I talk to her about my doubts for the sequence where the winning athlete is waiting to be executed. He's just understood how twisted the system that's trapped him is.

Véra reads the English text in silence. In the end, she types directly onto the document:

But actually, why should he speak if he knows he's going to die?

We're interrupted by someone knocking on the front door. We peek out of the window. Octave. Véra shoots me a sympathetic look, I'm still in my pyjamas, long woollen socks, hair uncombed. She tosses me one of her jumpers.

Octave has come to see what size trailer we'll need to take all the furniture to the rubbish tip. Tomorrow. He promised Véra he'd help. He looks at Véra's dressings, expresses his concern, then he looks around at the almost empty room and congratulates us. For some reason I'm irritated by his cheery tone. It seems forced. He avoids my gaze.

It takes all three of us to move the biggest pieces of furniture. The armoire and sofa are too heavy to lift so we slip some old sacking underneath them and slide them along the floor. The table is easier to move. We stack the chairs at the bottom of the steps. Upstairs, I stop Octave from opening the door to our parents' bedroom, I don't want him to see the bees. I'm worried about showing him our bunk beds but it turns out to be less embarrassing than I'd feared. We leave them where they are and just take the chest of drawers.

Before he goes, Octave gives us some chestnuts.

'We'll light the fire,' I say. 'Are you staying?'

He says he's sorry but he wants to go home and get his daughter's room ready. She's coming to stay for three days. He glances round the living room:

'You've got nothing left here. Come and stay at the château.'

Véra freezes. Then she declines the invitation, for both of us. She looks over at me before flashing Octave a smile.

The wood burns instantly, it's been drying for five years. We sit as close to the fire as we can, basking in the heat. Suddenly the room starts to fill with smoke, the chimney isn't drawing. We can't breathe. Sparks come flying out, spitting out insects that land across the room. We cover our noses and try and work out what's gone wrong. Véra fiddles with the vent, I go around opening doors and windows. Within five minutes the room is so cold Véra asks me to close them. Just then a shapeless lump of something coated in soot tumbles into the hearth. The smoke clears, the chimney seems to be working. I feel like dancing but Véra doesn't want to. She hands me a cookbook. She's opened it to a page with a recipe for liver served with onion confit made with Monbazillac wine. We bought some liver the other day at the supermarket. We'd been at the meat counter looking at tripe and wondering how you cook it. Neither of us had any idea and in the end we both felt rather turned off at the thought of eating it. I asked the young man at the counter all kinds of questions and I could see him growing impatient. When I said something about not being used to eating meat, he laughed and said he wasn't a big meat eater either and didn't really know much about it. My questions had stressed him out.

Véra takes the liver from its wrapper, handling it as delicately as if it were a baby bird emerging from its shell. The liver is smooth and shiny, like the paper it's wrapped in. She rinses away the blood from the wrapper and lays the liver back on top. I reach out and touch it, surprised at how firm it feels. Véra taps the countertop and flexes her bicep. Iron? My diet is fine, I say. I don't need any supplements. Well, she does, she tells me. I berate myself silently for being selfish. Véra rolls her eyes and points her knife at the recipe.

I read aloud:

'Cut the liver into strips. Place it to one side. Brown the onions in a little oil or duck fat.'

She's one step ahead of my instructions but I carry on reading regardless.

'Add the liver. Sprinkle with salt and pepper. Pour in the meat stock and Monbazillac wine.'

We don't have any. I produce a bottle of quince liqueur from the secret hiding place in the wall. Véra claps her hands and pours herself a glass. She stops and watches me pour one for myself. She raises her glass to say cheers but I can tell her mood has changed, her high spirits seem dampened.

We eat by the fire, sitting on a survival blanket I found near the boiler. The cooked liver has a crumbly texture. Rather like Irvin's sponge cake. I focus on the onions, trying not to think about the metallic taste. Véra brings us some water. Now that the living room has been cleared of all the furniture, I've noticed that we have a tendency to stay close to the wall. The ants, on the other hand, have taken to making their way across the room from one side to the other. I try and imagine what such a distance must seem like to these tiny creatures. They march in two columns as far as the piece of shrivelled lemon, then around and back again to where they started. I read on the internet that ants spend the winter deep underground.

'It's weird them being here, don't you think?' I say to Véra. She doesn't respond.

We sit as close as we can to the hearth. The chimney is drawing so well that even the heat gets sucked upwards. We eat some of the candied mandarins, chewing each bite for a long time, they're tough. Véra retreats into herself, her chin on her knees. She keeps clearing her throat. Swallowing irritates it. Absurdly, I think how strange it is for someone who doesn't speak to be unwell here. She pulls a packet of painkillers from her pocket and holds it up for me to see, then writes with a fine-nibbed felt-tip on the label:

`I'm stuffing myself with these.`

I try not to laugh out loud at her using the expression 'stuffing' herself. She wants me to try one too. The tablet coats my tongue, makes it feel cold and heavy. Véra doesn't need to use her tongue to articulate. I'm sure there was a time when I used to be envious of her silence but I can't remember when that was.

'You shouldn't lie on the floor the way you do.'

Véra protests. I insist. She gets annoyed.

'OK,' I sigh. 'You have the last word.'

She writes something.

Her last word, I think. Uttered at the age of six.

What was it? Something banal probably: 'no', 'why', 'OK'. Our first words are eagerly awaited, recorded for posterity. My friends with children make a ridiculous fuss about their offspring's utterances. But our last ones? The last word, something we always want to have, we never want to hear it from anyone else. But however hard I try, I can't remember the last thing she said. My memories of the days when Véra was still speaking are nothing but a jumble of impressions of the two of us and the world we lived in. I realise that now, even when I try and have a conversation with Véra in my head, she doesn't speak.

Véra hands me a scrap of paper.

`I take cold showers for your benefit, to protect you.`

'Protect me from what?' I ask bluntly.

I didn't realise I was using up all the hot water. I feel bad now about spending so long in the shower. Véra puts another log on the fire, throws the information leaflet for the pills into the flames.

'Do you think you'd have an accent?' I ask playfully, and then add, 'If you started speaking again one day, I mean.'

She makes a sound like a donkey braying.

Then, she writes on the floor with a charcoal pencil that's worn down to such a fine point she seems almost to be writing with her fingernails:

`If I wasn't your sister, would you be friends with me?`

I'm terrified of shattering the semblance of harmony we've arrived at. I ponder her question for ages, I want to give her an honest answer. No, I say as softly as I can, I don't think so. Véra's response comes as a complete surprise. She looks relieved. She wouldn't have believed me, she says, if I'd answered differently.

'What about you?'

She collects up the scraps of mandarin peel. Pulls a face, gives a disgusted look and sticks out her tongue at me. But her eyes are smiling.

The alcohol is making us pleasantly tipsy. I go into the bathroom to wash my hands. When I come out, Véra is standing first on one leg, then the other, moving her weight slowly from side to side, eyes closed. A performing bear, paws up, heavy-footed, balancing precariously. I place my hands on her waist, trying to follow her rhythm. Her bracelets clink together. I pick up the pace a little, try and get her to move with me. She falls into step. I press down on her hips, she bends her knees,

I fling her away, she jumps, makes a half-turn, arms wide, lands on one leg, the other leg raised behind her, head held high, her trousers all covered in dust. She holds the position for a few seconds, lowers her foot to the ground, curtseys and bows her head low, like a dancer.

13 NOVEMBER

The rubbish tip is just outside Nontron, a thirty-minute drive from our house. The road takes you through the forest and past ploughed fields until you get to the concrete wasteland of the industrial zone. Smoke from abattoirs rises high into the pale sky. Véra and I are in the orange van all piled up with boxes, Octave has gone ahead with our furniture. There's a chill in the air, the coldest it's felt since I've been here. Swann comes running over to us as soon as she sees us. From what I know of children, she seems tall for a five-year-old. Pointed chin, hamster-like profile, raincoat in the same shade of green as Octave's. Pretty, like her mother probably.

'How much does it hurt?' she asks Véra, pointing to the bandages.

They know each other. Véra pulls a face to make her laugh, Swann covers her eyes in sympathy, then shyly hands me a greasy package:

'Italian cornetti.'

She points out the different flavours: plain, almond cream, jam, hazelnut.

'We can eat them later,' Octave calls out from the trailer, shouting into the wind.

His voice is drowned out by the sound of a lorry pulling up. All four of us stand there open-mouthed for a few moments. The truck backs up against the container for scrap metal. The back of the truck rises, and with a thunderous roar the contents come crashing down. Swann blocks her ears. A mechanical arm, controlled by a man in a cabin that overhangs the container, breaks up the material and piles it all up for the bulldozer that shoves it all towards another container. Yellow machines, blue containers, colours that strike a false note. Fairground colours. They seem out of place here amid the din of destruction and the stench of decay.

At the far end of the site is an area where items in good condition are stocked, for people to help themselves. If no one takes them they're sent to charities who make good use of them. Octave says we've chosen a particularly busy day to come here. The site is closed most of the time, today is the first open day in a while. Cars line up. Lots of men on their own, boots, winter shirts, avoiding eye contact. I can see one couple, a family. A large woman, walking heavily, placing one foot, then the other. Making a visible effort. A man with gnarled hands is throwing out some empty cans. He peers inside them first as if to make sure they're really empty. Most people work quickly, vaguely ashamed. Hurrying to move on and let the next car in.

When our turn comes, we too work fast. We form a chain, pass cardboard, plastic, keeping an eye on Swann. Octave lifts with ease, his powerful body responding to whatever commands are running through his head. Véra and I work mechanically. I try and follow Octave's example, not stopping to think about the furniture being thrown into the tip. Amputated armchairs, broken tables, portraits of strangers. Swann walks towards us. It looks like monster soup, she says. I dump a bag of china onto a mattress. The great mechanical teeth descend. We draw back.

'Was that all in the cave?' Swann asks.

'It's not a cave, it's our house.'

I look over at Octave. He's all innocence.

'Octave says the doves are going to come back to the pigeonnier.'

'Pigeons,' I say, correcting her.

'Or doves,' Octave says. 'Pigeons, doves, they're all part of the Columbidae family.'

'Columbine!' says Swann. 'That's the statue.'

'The statue in the pond?' I reply.

She nods.

'Have you ever been into a cave?' I ask her.

'No.'

'Would you like to visit one?'

She opens her eyes wide. I think for a moment. We're not far from the Grotte de Villars. I know it's the only cave in the Périgord region to have stalactites and stalagmites as well as prehistoric paintings. My father did some work there twenty years ago. I remember an underground cavern with slender stalagmites. My father referred to it as the Candle Room. I google it to check, it closes tomorrow for the winter.

I mention it to Véra. She's busy throwing paper away. She pauses for a moment, surprised. Why not? Then she asks me to help her with the posters. The tarpaulin didn't give them enough protection from the rain. They're disintegrating into brightly coloured lumps. Before long our hands are coated in sticky mush. Swann comes to the rescue, using a piece of cardboard to scrape our fingers clean. Our school notebooks have grown stiff. The pages crumble, their texture somewhere between clay and parchment. Luckily the books were underneath them, they're in much better condition. We'll still be able to give them away.

'What are those mandala things anyway, the ones you were drawing on the posters?' I ask Véra.

She writes on a bit of card, her words aggressively underlined:

```
They're not mandalas, they're flowers. FLOWERS
that blossom in WINTER.
```

The depot section is not quite so noisy. People unfold items of clothing furtively, pick up the dishes, test their weight. As soon as we deposit our chairs, they're claimed by a man with two children. A woman asks Véra if there are moths in the sofa. Véra graces her with a smile and strokes the back of the sofa. The woman snorts and walks away. Véra sniffs in response. She strokes the fabric as if to smooth it out. Swann carries the lightest items, bags of my clothes. I notice something glinting. A sleeve embroidered with rhinestones hangs from one of the bags. It doesn't look familiar, it must be one that Véra bagged up. I wait for Swann to walk away and go over to take a closer look. My skating outfits. Rolled up carefully. I run my fingers over a pair of tights. They're still as soft as ever but my fingertips catch them a little. My skin, rough from the cold. Flaking around the nails, forming tiny little hooks.

'Do you want them?'

A woman is glaring at me. The one I noticed earlier, with the heavy legs. I fold the tights back up, say I was only looking at them. She grabs them and whisks the whole bag away.

In my mind the cave is always crowded with visitors – it was always summer when we went as children. But today, we seem to be the only ones here, apart from one other group, a family with three children. We wade through mud to get to the ticket office from the unpaved car park. Audio guides, no humans. Next to the ticket office there's a film being shown explaining how the terrain in this region was formed, how the caves were gouged out by underground rivers. To go down into the caves you walk along a tree-lined path and then enter a stone corridor lit from below. The audio guide, a woman's voice, welcomes us to the belly of the Dordogne, the cradle of prehistory. Swann walks ahead of me, between Octave and Véra. I feel a sense of responsibility, I really want her to like this place. The other children stare at Véra's dressings. Their father orders them to apologise to the lady. I don't like hearing Véra described as 'the lady'. I want to say something but Véra signals to me to let it go, it's not important. She starts play-acting, pretending to be a mummy and making the children giggle. Then she goes into making animal noises. The mother tells us to shush. The audio guide instructs us not to touch anything. Octave bends down to show Swann a stalactite hanging in front of the cave wall, she nods. I whisper to Véra: does she remember our stalagmite game when we were little? She knits her eyebrows. We used to spit on the ground, I say. Our father would get cross. I remind her of the caves at the Gouffre de Padirac. She waves her hand, of course she remembers the Gouffre, but the game, she can't picture it. She wants me to be quiet, she's listening to the audio guide. It's talking about the cavers discovering the site during the 1950s. I turn mine off.

Something is still bothering me. That memory, has Véra forgotten it? Did I make it up? I can see it so vividly, as clear as day. But if I have to carry the memory alone, I'd rather forget it.

The passageway narrows, we have to bend down as we walk. My heart races when we emerge into the cavern. There it is. The Candle Room. Stalactites and stalagmites, merged together to form columns, candles, even more numerous than in my memory, translucent. Actually, they look more to me as if they're made of ice.

'What are they?' Swann asks me.

I look over at Octave. He starts explaining about the colour of the stalactites, he says it's to do with water flowing through the earth, the faster it flows, the fewer sediments are left behind and the whiter the deposit remains. He winks at me, signalling to me that I should take over. Swann looks up at me. I improvise. I tell her that mountains are formed here, where we are standing. They take aeons to come into existence and grow so big, it takes unimaginable strength for them to rise up and reach for the sky. The oldest mountains are the ones that have broken through the earth's surface to tower above the people who live at their feet.

'So, in a way, we're living in a kind of incubator,' I say in conclusion.

'Like for chicks?'

I look over at Octave. He nods in agreement, then whispers to me:

'They have chickens at school.'

We arrive at the gallery with the cave paintings. We stand in front of what the audio guide informs us is 'one of the rare human manifestations of the prehistoric era'. A man, face to face with a bison. I hadn't remembered this image at all. The audio guide announces cheerily that we have reached the end of the visit and thanks us for our interest in this place that was inhabited by our Cro-Magnon ancestors 19,000 years ago. Swann bares her teeth. '*Croques mignons*,' she says, grinning. Sweet gnashers, a cross between croque monsieur and filet mignon. I force myself to smile at her little joke, feeling suddenly tense from the pain low down in my abdomen, the damp warmth that's started to leak. I'm afraid of it seeping through my clothes. I pull on my coat, laughing bitterly to myself. It's the same every month, I fail to recognise the signs, the bloating, the cravings, the black moods. It's only been a few months. How could I have forgotten so soon?

The door opens. We're dazzled by the blinding sunlight. Octave and Swann are the first to step outside, the group breaks up. Only now do I notice that Véra's not there. Swann must have been taking up all my attention. I retrace my steps, my heart in my mouth.

I find her in the Candle Room. Silhouetted, in profile, head turned up towards the ceiling, lost in thought.

'Are you coming?'

She signals to me that she'll be right behind me. I walk slowly back, listening for her footsteps behind me. Suddenly I turn round. She's standing, brushing a piece of rock lightly with her fingers.

The forest glows. Swann wants to wait for Véra, I walk ahead with Octave. Our hands are clammy from the humidity in the caves. He asks about my flight to New York. Am I all ready to go? What about Véra? Only half aware of what I'm saying, I tell him we're fine. It'll all work out.

In the souvenir shop, our hands feel dry again.

'We're definitely back in the land of the living,' Octave says. 'You can feel it on your skin.'

A few metres away, Swann and Véra are examining the fossils. Swann reaches up to say something in Véra's ear. Then Véra leans down towards Swann's ear. I can see her lips moving.

On the way out I can't resist the temptation to ask Swann: 'Did Véra speak to you?'

She murmurs, barely audibly, that she can't say, it's a secret.

It's dark when we get back. Before we do anything else we need to light the fire. Véra takes charge of this while I sweep upstairs for one last time. The house is empty except for the beds, our parents' bed anchored to the floor, and our bunkbeds, so flimsy on their spindly legs. A bee lies dead beside the door, its wings turned backwards. I sweep it into the dustpan with all the others and dump them all in the compost. As I work, I keep repeating to myself, like a mantra: 'I don't owe you anything, Papa; I love you, Véra and I don't owe you anything; I love you both, I owe you nothing.'

The hot water only lasts for three or four minutes. We shower together, wedged back-to-back. The water shoots out in sudden spurts. The hardest thing in the narrow shower cubicle is washing our hair. Raising our arms means we have to move closer together. My buttocks brush against Véra's.

'Sorry,' I mutter.

Véra puts her clothes back on. She wears a bra all the time. I fuss about her breasts being compressed. She shakes her head, I worry too much. I stare at her hair; it's just like mine, I hadn't noticed before. I usually have mine tied back in a ponytail. Now that we both have our hair down I can see the similarity. Hair like cotton wool.

I've brought our blankets downstairs and rolled them up with the survival blanket to make a nest for us. We spend the evening in it, melting the leftover bits of cheese onto bread rubbed with garlic. The fat drips onto the fire and creates a mini fireworks display. We roast some chestnuts, the smell gradually filling the room. I stroke their soft skin and enjoy the comforting sensation on my stomach of the hot water bottle that Véra's prepared for me. Véra goes to brush her teeth and I stretch out on the blanket. My phone vibrates. Irvin.

He misses me. He'll be there to meet me tomorrow.

I type out a message, delete it, try again several times. In the end I write:

It's Pickle Day tomorrow!

The ants march past close to my head. I place a glass in their path. The first few ants crash into it, but very quickly the column reforms and makes a detour around it. Through the bulge of the glass they take on huge monster-like proportions, shrinking back down to size as they emerge on the other side. I remove the glass and place my hand flat in their path. This time they don't try to go around the obstacle. The leader climbs up on my finger, the others follow, passing their loads from one ant to the next as they climb and marching all the way across my fingers, their bodies like the pearls of a delicate necklace.

Véra comes back down, sprawls across the blanket, I have to adjust my position. The fire has died down but I'm sweating. We smell of woodsmoke. Grease. I get up to go and find something to change into. The kitchen window is open, it doesn't close properly. I try and wedge it shut. Outside, a creature yelps. The sky looks stormy. Wind in the alder trees. My cramps have got worse. I reheat the hot water bottle. Véra doesn't seem to be sweating. She's lying curled up in a ball, knees to chin, her body solid as a rock. She's moved over to make space for me. I try and get back to sleep. After a few moments I feel a slight quivering at my back. I turn over, touch my hand to her shoulder. My hand is hot again, dry. The shaking stops, then starts up again, more intensely. Véra draws her knees in tighter to her chest. I stroke her cheek. It feels damp. I move my hand down to the curve of her hips, press lightly. Véra places it on her stomach, enfolds my hand in hers.

We lie there for a long time, not moving. Spasmodic gulps give way to long, deep breaths. Véra's hand flops back down. She draws it up to rest close to her neck. Rain spatters against the windowpane.

14 NOVEMBER

Late morning, milky sunlight. Wind-blown leaves have covered the statue, obscured her grainy skin; only her face remains visible, turned towards the water. Véra and I kneel beside the pond, wondering if this is all a dream. Beneath the surface of the water, plants coil together. A shape emerges, like a clover leaf, the size of a face. We've never seen it in this pond before. The green shines so vividly against the peat, it seems phosphorescent. Bare trees, their reflections shimmering, clothed in green. As if they're trying on their new leaves for spring.

Véra stands up. Suddenly, just at the spot where the statue's gaze is focused, the water turns cloudy. We watch as the key to our house sinks, its descent barely slowed by the fresco of leaves waving beneath the ripples that stretch in ever-widening circles all the way to the water's edge, shaking the image of the château on the hill and making it tremble.

My father would have us believe that nothing was reflected in the blackness of the pond, not even the stars. I know, of course, that he was making it up. All bodies of water cast reflections of the universe when light shines on them. Véra and I are so unsettled by the vision of these leaves in the water that we both look up together and gaze at the trees, the hillside, the château, as if to confirm that they really are there.

My sister takes my hand as I stand up alongside her. Is she steadying herself or offering to support me? One way or the other, I'm certain she is thinking the same as I am. It's time to leave. Go back to the house. Pick up our suitcases, embrace one another on the steps and go our separate ways. We will close the door for the last time and go down the hill, leaving the house unlocked, the shutters open, curtains undrawn. Our house is not a ruin, it never will be. Its stones will be used again to provide, as they always have, a place of shelter. And as we leave, the image of the pigeonnier will be there still, reflected in the pond, a watchtower guarded by those to whom we turn to bid farewell.

DAUNT BOOKS

Founded in 2010, Daunt Books Publishing grew out of Daunt Books, independent booksellers with shops in London and the south of England. We publish the finest writing in English and in translation, from literary fiction – novels and short stories – to narrative non-fiction, including essays and memoirs. Our modern classics list revives authors whose work has unjustly fallen out of print. In 2020 we launched Daunt Books Originals, an imprint for bold and inventive new writing.

www.dauntbookspublishing.co.uk

We ensure all our products comply with GPSR, CE marking, and other applicable EU Directives. Our EU Responsible Person for GPSR product safety compliance is EU Compliance Partner.

EU Responsible Person (EU RP):
EU Compliance Partner

Postal address: Pärnu mnt. 139b – 14, 11317 Tallinn, Estonia

Contact Email: hello@eucompliancepartner.com

Website: www.eucompliancepartner.com

Phone: +33757690241